Chances and Changes

My Journey with Molly

by Valerie Tripp

American Girl®

Published by American Girl Publishing

18 19 20 21 22 23 QP 10 9 8 7 6 5 4 3 2 1

Cover image by David Roth and Juliana Kolesova

Cataloging-in-Publication Data available from the Library of Congress

To Beverly Dawson and Barbara Peck Rothrock,
with gratitude for your help

Beforever™

The adventurous characters you'll meet in
the BeForever books will spark your curiosity
about the past, inspire you to find your voice
in the present, and excite you about your future.
You'll make friends with these girls as you share
their fun and their challenges. Like you, they are
bright and brave, imaginative and energetic,
creative and kind. Just as you are, they are
discovering what really matters: Helping others.
Being a true friend. Protecting the earth.
Standing up for what's right. Read their stories,
explore their worlds, join their adventures.
Your friendship with them will BeForever.

A Journey Begins

This book is about Molly, but it's also about a girl like you who travels back in time to Molly's world of 1945. You, the reader, get to decide what happens in the story. The choices you make will lead to different journeys and new discoveries.

When you reach a page in this book that asks you to make a decision, choose carefully. The decisions you make will lead to different endings. (Hint: Use a pencil to check off your choices. That way, you'll never read the same story twice.)

Want to try another ending? Go back to a choice point and find out what happens when you make different choices.

Before your journey ends, take a peek into the past, on page 166, to discover more about Molly's time.

1

Are you sure, Margaret?" My friend Beatriz DiMichael asks. Her fingers are poised over the keyboard, ready to mark our final choice.

I look at the list on the screen one more time and nod slowly. But as Bea highlights the name we've agreed on, I suddenly change my mind.

"Well, maybe not."

"Margaret Maybe!" Bea laughs, calling me by her nickname for me. "I *knew* you hadn't decided yet!"

I laugh, too. My best friend knows me too well. I hate making decisions. "Naming a new horse is important," I say. "Your horse, Aurora, is having a foal and we're picking the name her foal will have its whole life!"

Bea rolls her eyes. "This is as bad as waiting for you to choose which instrument you wanted to play," she says. "You had to try every single one in the orchestra before you decided."

I grin thinking about that month at the beginning of school last year. "I *did* take a long time to choose," I admit. "But it was worth the wait. I love playing the flute."

"And you're really good at it, too," says Bea. "But

Aurora is going to have this foal any minute, so we need to . . ."

"Make a decision," we say at the same time.

Bea prints a copy of the name list and hands it to me. "Take this home and think about it," she says with a smile. "We're going to have the best summer ever. It'll be worth the wait, too."

"Absolutely," I agree. "There's no maybe about that."

The screen door to Bea's house closes quietly behind me, and my dog, Barney, who has been dozing on the front porch, lifts his head. "Come on, Barney," I say.

Barney and I walk through the woods between Bea's family farm and our house at the ranger station. My grandmother, Gem, and I live in Seneca Forest Preserve where Gem is the wildlife ranger. I love it here, especially summers. Bea is homeschooled, and I go to the public school in town, so all year we look forward to spending our summer days together and sleeping over at each other's houses most nights. We help Gem maintain the trails in the preserve and care for sick or injured wild animals. We also help take care of the animals on Bea's farm, and we swim in the lake every day, rain or shine.

Swimming is my favorite summer tradition, but this summer there's something I'm looking forward to even more: helping to raise a foal! Aurora is Bea's horse, so this foal will be ours to raise. I can't wait to watch it grow.

I arrive home to find a letter addressed to me propped up on my music stand. I put down the list of horse names and pick up the long white envelope. The return address reads, "Young Artists' Summer Music Camp."

What can this be?

✪ ***Turn to page 4.***

I open the envelope carefully and read the letter. Twice. I can't quite believe it. Suddenly, Gem's voice makes me jump.

"You found your mail!" she says. "What did you get from the—" But Gem stops short when she sees my face. "Is something wrong?" she asks.

"No," I say slowly. "Not wrong, just really surprising. I've been offered a scholarship to a summer music camp. It begins next week."

"What?" Gem says. "May I see?"

I hand her the letter. As she reads it, I say, "The letter says that my orchestra teacher, Mr. Salvo, nominated me. He sent the admissions committee a video of our last concert."

"The one with your fantastic solo," Gem says.

"The solo I almost didn't do," I say. "I couldn't decide if I was ready to play on my own in front of an audience or not. I was so nervous."

"You were *amazing*," says Gem. "I was proud of you then, and I'm proud of you now." Gem hugs me. "A scholarship! Congratulations, Margaret. You are going to have an unforgettable summer."

I fold the letter and put it back in the envelope.

"What's the matter, sweetie?" Gem asks. "You don't look happy about this great news."

"I'm not sure I want to go to music camp," I say. "Bea and I have a lot of plans for this summer. And I've never been away from home for so long. Maybe—"

"This is no time for maybes," Gem interrupts. "An opportunity like music camp doesn't come along every day."

I pick up the list of names for Aurora's foal. *Neither does the chance to raise a foal,* I think.

✪ ***Turn to page 6.***

✪ 6 ✪

I toss and turn all night, wondering, *What should I do?*

The phone rings just before seven A.M. It's Bea. "Come over," she says. "Right away!"

Barney and I race through the woods. Bea is waiting for me at the edge of the pasture, and she practically drags me to the barn, putting her hands over my eyes just as we walk in. Then Bea takes her hands away from my eyes and says, "You can look now."

It's dark in the barn, so at first all I see is a shaft of sunlight. As my eyes adjust, I see Bea's mare, Aurora, and—"Oh!" I gasp. "Aurora had her foal!"

Gem is in the stall, calmly stroking Aurora's sweaty neck. Gem has helped at the births of hundreds of animals, both wild and tame. "Bea called me at five this morning," Gem says. "But by the time I got here, Aurora had already done all the hard work."

Bea and I hug. We stand outside the stall staring silently at the foal. Aurora looks over her shoulder at us, then nudges her spindly-legged, shiny black foal as if to say, *Go meet the girls. They're my old friends.* The foal wobbles. It can't quite figure out how to coordinate all four legs, which are as stiff and skinny as stilts, so it stands still, looking puzzled.

"Never mind," Bea tells the foal. "Stay put. We can admire you from here."

"Hello, Aurora's foal," I say. "Hello—"

"Moon Shadow," Bea and I say at exactly the same moment.

"That's the perfect name," I say.

Bea nods. Then she says to Gem, "We had a list of about a million others."

"We talked about the name for months, every day," I add.

"And now, every day, we can watch Moon Shadow grow," says Bea happily.

Gem and I exchange a look. My heart twists. "Bea," I say slowly, "I'm not sure I'll be here every day."

"Why not?" asks Bea.

"I found out yesterday that I've been offered a scholarship to a music camp," I say. "It begins next week."

"Oh, Margaret. That's great!" says Bea. "Good for you! And don't worry, you'll still have lots of time with Moon Shadow. You can come over in the mornings, before camp, and afternoons, after camp, right?"

I shake my head. "It's a sleep-away camp."

"Oh," says Bea. "Two weeks?"

"Eight," I say softly.

"That's the whole summer!" says Bea, dismayed.

I try to say something but I can't. So I just nod.

"You can't go," Bea says passionately. "We've waited *all year* for summer. Moon Shadow is finally here, and we have so many great plans. I need your help."

"I'll be here to help," Gem says kindly.

Bea sighs. "Thank you, but it won't be the same. Besides, you're busy taking care of the preserve."

"I'll be fine," says Gem. "Mischa's here to help me."

Gem's words sting a bit. A few weeks ago, Mischa swooped in and came to stay in our ranger station. He's a forestry student who is doing a summer internship with Gem. He took over some of things *I* do without even *asking* me. I can't wait until his internship is done and he leaves.

But Gem is still talking about *me* leaving. She says, "It's time for Margaret to try something new. Music camp is a great opportunity for her. And it's eight weeks, not forever."

"But it's right now," says Bea. She turns to me.

"You'd miss Moon Shadow's first two months. You'd miss home. You'd miss swimming. You'd miss *everything.*"

I look over at the stall, where Moon Shadow is nestled close to Aurora. Oh, how I wish I didn't have to make this decision!

"I'd miss *you,*" Bea says. "You're my best friend. What will I do without you?"

"I haven't decided about camp yet," I say. "Maybe I'll go and maybe I won't."

"Margaret Maybe," says Bea, sighing. "You do hate to make decisions, don't you?"

✪ ***Turn to page 10.***

10

Gem invites Bea over for homemade waffles, but Bea says she's not hungry. So Gem and I go home to breakfast and a conversation full of maybes. I'm no closer to a decision when Barney lifts his head and barks.

Mischa walks in, and Gem says, "Good morning, Mischa. If you're hungry, help yourself to some waffles."

"Thanks," says Mischa. He scratches Barney's ears, and Barney thumps his tail happily. Those two were friends the moment they met. "What do you know, Margaret Jo?" Mischa asks, sitting down next to me. He always says that, and it drives me crazy.

I get up and say, "I'm going to take a walk and clear my head."

"Is there anything I can do to help?" Mischa asks.

No, nosy Mischa! I want to say. But I just shake my head. "Come on, Barney," I call. But Barney's settled in next to Mischa. *Fine,* I think.

I meander through the woods, alone. Usually, when I've got a problem, I ask Gem or Bea for advice. But this time, they *are* my problem. Gem thinks I should go to music camp. Bea thinks I should stay home. Not only can I not decide what I want to do, but whatever choice I make is going to disappoint one of them.

After walking for a long time, I flop down on some rotting wooden steps that I've never noticed before. The steps lead nowhere, which is appropriate because so far, my thinking's leading nowhere, too. One minute I have this itchy urge to go to music camp and try something new, and the next minute I think, *No way! I am not leaving home this summer of all summers.* Argh!

There's a breeze in the treetops, but the morning sun is getting hot. I glance at my watch to see how late it's getting, and as I do, I see something shiny on the ground. It's jewelry—a gold pin with one white stone and three red stones, probably dropped by a hiker. I pick it up and rub the dirt off the white stone. *Whoosh!* First there's darkness, then glaring sunlight.

✪ ***Turn to page 12.***

12

When my eyes focus again, things look different. The steps aren't rotted anymore, and now they lead up to a big wooden building behind me that's labeled "Dining Hall." Where on earth did *that* come from, and how come the steps look new?

I look at the pin. Everything was normal until I rubbed the white stone. But before I can figure out what's happened, I hear a girl say, "Hi!"

Shoving the pin in my pocket, I turn to face her. "Uh, hi?" I say.

"You must be a new camper," the girl says. "Welcome to Camp Gowonagin!"

Camp what? Am I dreaming? Is this girl real?

She smiles, and it's the most real smile I've ever seen. "I'm Molly," she says. With old-fashioned politeness, she holds out her hand to shake mine and says, "How do you do? What's your name?"

"Margaret," I manage to mumble, wondering where I am. I look around. Beside the Dining Hall, a wide, shady path winds up a hill. There are tan tents on one side of the hill, and on the other side green fields slope down to a border of dark green pine trees. A sparkling lake peeks through the trees. Everywhere, I see chattering groups of girls greeting each other happily. Most of them are dressed like Molly, in white shirts, red shorts, and red caps.

I grip the steps for dear life because I am so dizzy. As impossible as it seems, somehow I am at a girls' summer camp. What just happened?

My face must look as mixed up and scared as I feel, because Molly says kindly, "Camp is sort of overwhelming on the very first day, I know. But you'll love it! I promise. The camp director, Miss Butternut, is really nice and so are all the counselors." Her face brightens. "I know what!" she says. "I'll introduce you to my friend Linda. Wait here a second while I run inside the Dining Hall and get her."

Molly takes the steps two at a time, her long brown braids bouncing on her back as she bounds past me up the steps. As the screen door swings shut behind her, I slip my hand into my pocket, take out the pin, and look at it. What will happen if I rub it again? Will it take me home?

✪ ***Turn to page 14.***

14

Unusually for me, I make an instant decision. I rub the pin again. And again, after a whoosh of darkness, I blink in the light. This time I'm back in my own woods, sitting on the splintery steps, the pin in my hand. I look at my watch, and no time has passed!

I'm relieved to be home. But then I begin to think. I liked Molly. She was so friendly and welcoming. Being with her felt good: It was a break from worrying about my big decision. *Here's a golden opportunity to find out what it's like to go someplace new,* I think. The part of me that itches for adventure wants to go back to Molly. So even though I'm not sure where the pin will take me, I make another impulsive decision. I rub the pin again, hoping it will bring me back to Molly.

I whoosh though darkness, blink in bright sunshine, and hooray! I find myself sitting on the new-looking steps again. When I turn around, Molly and another girl in a camp uniform are coming down the steps. I put the pin in my pocket to keep it safe and stand up.

"This is Linda," says Molly. "And this," she says, patting my shoulder, "is Margaret, like Princess Margaret in England."

"Also like Margaret Truman," says Linda. "You know, President Truman's daughter."

"President Truman," Molly says, shaking her head. "I still can't get used to saying that. The president has *always* been Franklin Roosevelt my whole life."

Whoa. This talk of princesses and presidents has me completely confused. Truman is not the president. Not now! Then it hits me: I'm not just in another *place*; I'm in another *time*. The pin I found has transported me back to the past! I feel terrified and excited at the same time.

Linda's asking me a question. "Don't you think it's unfair that President Roosevelt didn't live to see V-E Day, the end of the war in Europe?"

I rack my rattled brains, trying to remember my American history so that I can figure out what year I'm in. We learned that Franklin Roosevelt led the United States out of the Great Depression in the 1930s and nearly to the end of World War Two. Roosevelt died suddenly, and his vice president, Harry Truman, took over. That means I have traveled back to 1945!

✪ ***Turn to page 16.***

Linda is saying, "It's just so sad that Roosevelt won't be around to celebrate when the soldiers come home." She turns to Molly. "You must be glad that *your* dad already came home, Molly. I bet it's wonderful now that everything at your house is back to the way it was before the war."

"Yes," Molly says quietly. A funny look crosses her face, as if something about home is not quite wonderful. But she quickly shakes it off and looks at me. "Where's *your* home, Margaret?" she asks.

"I live with my grandmother, Gem, in a forest preserve," I explain. "Gem's a wildlife ranger. She knows all about taking care of wild animals like raccoons and deer, and farm animals, like my friend's horse, Aurora."

Linda gapes. "You have a *horse*?" she asks.

"My friend Bea does," I say. "Bea and her family have a farm right next to the forest preserve." I add wistfully, "Aurora just had a foal."

"Oh, a *foal*!" sighs Linda, enchanted.

"Wow!" says Molly. "If you live in a forest, you must know all about wilderness survival and camping."

"Camping, maybe," I say. "But camp, no. I've never been to summer camp before."

I must sound worried, because Molly puts a comforting arm around my shoulder and says, "You'll feel better once you settle in. You can stay with us in Tent Ten."

"That's a great idea," says Linda. "There's an empty bed in our tent. Now you can use it."

"We'll help you move in," says Molly. "Where's your trunk?"

Uh oh. I don't *have* a trunk. "Uh, I . . . I," I stammer.

Linda asks, "Is it lost?"

"I'm sure it's just late, not lost," says Molly. "That happened to a girl last summer. It'll turn up." She reassures me, "Don't worry, Margaret. We'll lend you clothes to wear until your trunk arrives."

"But what about a bathing suit and pajamas and something to keep her stuff in?" asks Linda.

Molly's not fazed for an instant. "We can find everything for Margaret in the Lost and Found," she says. "Let's go."

"This is going to be fun," says Linda, "like shopping, but for free."

✪ ***Turn to page 18.***

B*eep, beep!* A blue car honks at us as we're walking toward the Lost and Found. The driver waves and calls in a cheery voice, "Molly!"

"Dad?" says Molly. She runs to the car, and Linda and I follow her. "Is everything okay?"

"Everything's fine, olly Molly. You just forgot this," says Molly's dad. He gets out of the car and hands Molly a pillow.

"Thanks, Dad!" says Molly, hugging her father. "It was awfully nice of you to drive back with this."

"Well, I was only partway home when I saw it in the backseat, so I turned right around," he says. He smiles lovingly at Molly and gives one of her braids a gentle tug. Then he turns to Linda. "Hi, there, Linda!"

"Hi, Dr. McIntire," says Linda. She nods toward me. "This is our friend, Margaret. She's a new camper."

"Nice to meet you, Margaret," says Dr. McIntire. "I hope you like Camp Gowonagin as much as Linda and Molly do. It's a good break for you kids. The war's hard on you, too." He pretends be serious. "Doctor's orders: Promise me that you'll have as much fun as possible."

"Okay!" say all three of us.

"And all kidding aside, be sure to stick together if

you go hiking," Dr. McIntire says. "Look out for one another—especially in the water."

"We will," says Linda.

Dr. McIntire hugs Molly one more time and gets back into the car. "I'm heading for home—again. Or as you campers would say, I'm going to 'go on agin.'"

We all laugh, but I think Molly looks sad as she waves and says, "Good-bye, Dad."

"Good-bye!" calls Dr. McIntire.

"Molly, next to mine, your dad is the nicest dad in the whole world," says Linda.

Molly nods. "I know," she says. She sighs. "That just makes it worse."

Now I'm sure Molly looks sad. "What's worse?" I ask.

"Nothing," Molly says briskly. "Never mind. Let's go."

What's the matter with Molly? I wonder. *Is she sorry to say good-bye to her father? Or is it something else that has made her eyes look so full of woe?*

✪ ***Turn to page 20.***

20

The Lost and Found is in the attic of the Recreation Hall. As Molly leads the way, she and Linda say hello to everyone we pass. I can only manage a nervous smile. I'm still struggling to make sense of what's happened, and I feel like the awkward new girl. I don't know anyone—or anything—here at Camp Gowhatchamacallit.

We thunder up a set of steps, and in no time I'm fitted out in a uniform just like Molly's and Linda's. I'm wearing red shorts, a white shirt, a blue scarf tied at my neck, and a red cap. As I slip my gold pin into my shorts pocket, Molly notices that the shorts are a little loose around the waist, so she bunches my shirt up in the back and tucks it in. "There!" she says. "Perfect!"

"Here are some pajamas, and a rucksack to keep your stuff in," Linda says, handing me an army green bag. I start putting my other clothes, and the swimming suit Molly found for me, in the bag when I notice Linda looking at my neon green running shoes with pink fluorescent laces. "Where'd you get those shoes?" she asks. "I've never seen anything like those before."

That's because they won't exist for another seventy years, I think.

"Here," Molly says, handing me a pair of blue-and-white saddle shoes. "Try these."

I'm reluctant to give up my running shoes. But when I put the saddle shoes on, I'm glad, partly because the saddle shoes are cool in a hipster sort of way, but mostly because Linda says, "*Now* you look like a camper." She bursts into song, and Molly joins in:

Welcome to Camp Gowonagin!
We're mighty glad you're here!
Hooray! Hooray! For Gowonagin!
Hail! Hail! Let's give a cheer!

✪ ***Turn to page 22.***

✪ 22 ✪

"I *am* mighty glad you're here, Margaret," says Molly. "I can't wait to teach you all the Camp Gowonagin songs and cheers."

"And traditions," Linda adds. "Like campfires and ghost stories and All Wet Day."

"Oh, I *love* the water," I say.

"Then you'll love being at camp," Linda says. "We swim every day."

"Margaret might love the overnight hike, too," Molly says, nodding toward a sleeping bag, canteen, and a small aluminum pot with a lid that she calls a mess kit. "She could use these."

"Hike?" I ask. That's something I know how to do.

"It's a two-night camping trip into the woods that ends up at a secret pond," Molly explains. "We weren't old enough to go last summer."

"It'd be us on the hike, and some other campers, and some counselors, too," says Linda. "But there's only one chance to go, and the group leaves today."

Molly turns to me. "Which would *you* like to do, Margaret?" she asks. "Go on the hike or stay at camp?"

Go or stay? That question *again*. I know that Molly is being polite by asking my opinion, but she doesn't know how much I hate making decisions, especially when *both* choices sound great.

"I'm terrible at making decisions," I say. "I hate to disappoint anyone. My friend Bea calls me Margaret Maybe. I know it's annoying to be wishy-washy, but—"

Molly interrupts. "It's not annoying," she says nicely. "It just means you look before you leap. My mom *always* tells me to do that. It's good to stop and think before you act."

"Yes," agrees Linda, in a brisk, straightforward way. "If you *don't* stop to think about what other people might want, *that's* annoying."

"I never thought of it that way!" I grin.

"Linda and I are going to be happy no matter what you choose," says Molly.

Linda nods in agreement. "Tell us what *you* want to do."

✪ ***To go on the hike,***
turn to page 27.

✪ ***To stay at camp,***
turn to page 24.

24

This is my chance to find out what summer camp is like! I love to swim, so All Wet Day sounds like fun, and boy-oh-boy, haven't I been bounced around enough today? So I say, "How about staying here?"

"Hooray!" cheer Molly and Linda.

"I was hoping you'd choose that, Margaret," says Molly.

"Me, too," says Linda. "All Wet Day is all *kinds* of fun."

"Linda's part fish," Molly explains.

Linda sucks in her cheeks and purses her lips to make a fish face.

"I'm a mermaid myself," I joke. "My friend Bea and I have a tradition of swimming every day in the summer, rain or shine. My hair stays wet from May to October."

"Oh, no, not you, too," Molly pretends to groan. "Now I have two friends who are fishy."

Linda grins at me. "I knew you and I would get along *swimmingly*," she puns.

"Good one," I say.

"Thanks!" says Linda.

"You're *whale-come,*" I say.

"You two are terrible!" chuckles Molly. "Come on. We'd better hurry to our tent and make up Margaret's bunk. Pretty soon Miss Butternut will blow the bugle for All Camp Meeting."

"The bugle?" I ask as we walk quickly up the hill to Tent Ten.

"Yes," Linda explains. "Miss Butternut's bugle is our clock at camp."

"She blows it to wake us up in the morning," says Molly. She and Linda sing to the tune of "Reveille":

I can't get 'em up,
I can't get 'em up,
I can't get 'em up
in the morning.

"The day is divided up into activities, like arts and crafts, nature class, archery, horseback riding, team sports, and swimming," Linda explains. "The bugle blows at the beginning and end of every activity, and before and after every meal."

"Speaking of meals, sometimes you have to bring a

letter you've written to mail home to the Dining Hall or you won't be allowed in for the meal," says Molly. "But don't worry. You can use a piece of my stationery. I packed a whole box of writing paper in my trunk."

My mind's boggling at bugles and letters-for-meals. "You're kidding," I say. Camp Gowonagin sounds so regimented and strict! I ask, "Is camp run like the army or something?"

Molly and Linda look completely serious. "Well, yes," they say. "How else?"

Then I remember that it's 1945, and World War Two is still going on. Rules and regulations make sense to everyone—even kids at summer camp.

✪ *Turn to page 28.*

I feel happy and at home in the woods, so I choose the hike. Molly and Linda are both thrilled, which is a relief.

"Margaret, you have what you need," Molly says, picking up the sleeping bag, canteen, and mess kit. "But Linda and I need to get our gear. Come on."

I pick up the rucksack and follow.

"I can't *wait* to see the secret pond," Linda says as we clatter down the stairs from the Lost and Found and run across camp to Tent Ten. "I'm so glad you chose the hike, Margaret."

"Me, too," Molly says. "All Wet Day is *not* going to be my finest hour."

"Why not?" I ask.

"Swimming isn't Molly's favorite thing," says Linda. "Neither is diving."

"Diving," Molly repeats. She has that same worried look she had when her dad was here. Then she says, "Let's hurry. The hike is starting soon."

✪ ***Turn to page 31.***

Tent Ten is so cool! It's bigger than I thought it would be—big enough to stand in. Inside, bunk beds are lined up military-style on either side, with tidy trunks or duffel bags at the foot of each. The tent is also much friendlier and cozier than I imagined an army tent would look. The tent flaps are rolled up and fastened so that the sides are open to the fresh air. Girls are playing jacks, making up their beds, and hanging their clothes on hooks. I feel shy when I see all the new faces turn toward me, but every face is friendly—and just about everyone knows Molly and Linda.

"Molly! Linda! Welcome back!" The girls cheer. They jump up and hug Molly and Linda, and break out clapping and chanting:

Linda, Molly: they're true blue,
They are campers through and through,
They are campers, and they say:
Three cheers for Camp Gowonagin,
Hooray, Hooray, Hooray!

Molly says, "Hello, everybody. This is Margaret.

This is her first time at camp."

"Hi, Margaret!" say all the girls, smiling and making me feel welcome. Molly introduces me to Nancy, Carolyn, and Edie. They introduce us to Bobbie, a new camper. When Linda tells the girls about my missing trunk, they all offer to loan me anything I might need. They're so nice!

Molly also introduces me to a counselor-in-training, Betty, who'll sleep in our tent with us, and Miss Archer, one of the senior counselors. The counselors are helping Bobbie unpack her trunk.

Molly and Linda help me make my bed, which is good because it takes three of us to tuck the sheets in properly. "They have to be pulled tight enough so that you could bounce a quarter off them," explains Linda. "Just like in the army."

Toot-a-loot! The bugle blasts. I jump a foot, startled by how loud the bugle is, but everyone else cheers, and I'm swept up in the stampede of girls. We all dash out of the tent, take the steps in a leap, and race down the path to the Dining Hall.

It's noisy in the Dining Hall! All of us in Tent Ten sit at the same table, but we have to shout at one another to be heard. Girls are shrieking hellos to one another and laughing, and pretty soon *everyone* is singing:

Welcome to Gowonagin!
We're mighty glad you're here!
We'll send the air reverberating with a mighty cheer!
We'll sing you in, we'll sing you out.
We will raise a mighty shout:
Hail, Hail Gowonagin!
Gowonagin, Hoo-rah, HOO-RAH!!

That line about sending "the air reverberating with a mighty cheer" is totally true, no exaggeration. They sure do like to sing here at Camp Gowonagin. The whole scene is chaotic until . . .

✪ ***Turn to page 33.***

We run up a hill to Tent Ten, which is built on a wooden platform with a wide front step. While Molly and Linda hurry to collect their camping stuff, I sit on the step and catch my breath. I wonder what Bea is doing right now. I hate knowing I have made her sad and worried.

Molly and Linda appear with their gear, which looks just like the stuff I got from the Lost and Found: old-fashioned! Our sleeping bags are scratchy woolen bedrolls tied with leather belts. Molly shows me how to attach it to my rucksack, and she helps me hoist the bundle on my back. *Yikes*, I think. *It's heavy.*

We head back down the hill and across the camp, stopping at the Dining Hall to fill our canteens. We meet the rest of the group that has chosen to go on the hike at the trailhead. There are two counselors, Barbara and Judy, and five other campers. Molly introduces me to Patty, Kathy, Marie, Shirley, and Dorinda. They were all at camp last year, and I realize I'm the only girl who doesn't know all the Camp Gowonagin songs and traditions.

Molly sees that I'm feeling a bit lost. "Don't worry," she says kindly. "None of us have been on the overnight hike. It's new for all of us."

Before we leave, the counselors set some ground rules. "Stick together," Judy says. "Don't go off on your own."

I nudge Molly and say, "That's what your dad said. Stick together."

Molly nods. "Army rules," she says. "Soldiers always look out for one another."

Barbara holds up an old-fashioned walkie-talkie. "I can communicate back and forth with camp in an emergency," she says. "But we'll be fine. I won't need to use this, right campers?" she asks.

"Right!" everyone responds.

And with that, we're off.

✪ ***Turn to page 35.***

33

*T**oo-oot!* That must be Miss Butternut, the camp director, blowing the bugle. Everyone wiggles and whispers and finally gets quiet.

"Welcome, old campers and new campers. I'm sure that this will be the best summer ever at Camp Gowonagin!" says Miss Butternut.

Once again, the room explodes with cheers. Immediately, I think of Bea and how we were planning to have *our* "best summer ever." I miss Bea!

"Now, girls, as some of you know, one of our favorite camp traditions is All Wet Day," says Miss Butternut.

"Hooray!" erupt all the old campers, whooping so wildly that Miss Butternut has to blow her bugle again and then flap her hands to get everyone to settle down.

"All of you will be in your bathing suits all day on All Wet Day, because you'll all be all wet all day," says Miss Butternut, getting all tangled up in her explanation. "There are fun games for *everyone* like bubble-blowing, the bucket brigade, and the water slide."

The room erupts into cheers again, and Miss Butternut cheers along, her gray curls bouncing as if they're electrified.

"We've added something new this year that I know you'll love," Miss Butternut says when the room quiets down. "A swim meet! Those who wish to may compete, even if they're only at the Pollywog Level and don't dive or swim underwater yet."

Linda and I look at each other and grin. "I want to swim in the meet," Linda says.

"Me, too," I say. "I love to swim!"

Molly looks serious when she says, "It'll only be fun if all three of us do the same thing."

"The meet *will* be fun," Linda reassures her. "Don't worry. Miss Butternut said even Pollywogs can compete."

Molly's a Pollywog? I think. But I don't have time to ask her about it, because Miss Butternut says, "All right! Anyone who wants to be in the swim meet should gather at the lake in five minutes—all suited up. Off you go, girls."

✪ ***Turn to page 37.***

35

We hike single-file on a narrow trail. I'm surprised to hear the campers start singing, "Great green gobs of greasy, grimy gopher guts." I have to laugh. Bea and I sing that when we have a messy chore to get through. Now here I am, in 1945, singing the same song. Mr. Salvo, my orchestra teacher, is always saying that music is a language that is timeless. I guess he's right. We all sing really loudly as we hike along, our mess kits clanking against our canteens, our bedrolls bouncing cheerfully on our backs, and the hot, sultry air making us sweat.

When we come to a burbling little stream, Barbara shows us stepping-stones we can use to cross. Shirley, Kathy, Patty, and Dorinda follow her, but daredevil Marie asks, "Can I cross on this log instead?"

"Sure," say Barbara and Judy. They let Marie go ahead, grinning as she shrieks and squeaks every step of the slippery way and then scrambles up the muddy bank on the other side.

Molly and Linda, holding their arms out from their sides for balance, cross on the log, too, and I make my teetery way behind them. When I get to the other side, Molly and Linda lean down to pull me up the steep bank, shouting, "Oops-a-daisy!" and laughing as we all tumble together in a tangled pile.

"Thanks!" I pant.

"You won't thank them if that's poison ivy you've landed in," says Dorinda as we scramble to our feet in a bunch of greenery.

"It isn't," says Molly. "Poison ivy has three leaves. Believe me, I know poison ivy when I see it."

"This is myrtle," I say. "It grows wild near streams like this."

"Margaret knows all about everything in the wilderness," says Molly proudly, thumping me on the back. "She lives in a forest preserve."

"Neato!" says Marie. "That must be wonderful."

"It is," I say. I take a deep breath. The scents of pine-sap, moss, and sun-warmed earth remind me of home. Bea is right: I'd miss home if I went to music camp.

✪ ***Turn to page 39.***

37

We hurry to Tent Ten to change into our bathing suits. I fold my shorts carefully so that my pin doesn't fall out of the pocket, and then I pull on the bathing suit I got from Lost and Found. My suit! It is so *weird*. It has two skinny straps that tie in a bow behind my neck. It puckers out over my hips and is gathered in the back in pleats. To top it all off, the crowning touch to my comical swimming outfit is a rubber bathing cap with a tight chin strap that snaps at the side. I look like a clown. Bea would laugh out loud if she could see me! This is *not* how we look in our sleek tank suits when we swim every day in the summer! I feel ridiculous, but when we get down to the waterfront, I see that everyone else at the lake is suited and capped just as I am.

"Stay inside the ropes!" shouts Miss Archer. "Old campers, buddy up with new campers and explain how the Buddy Board works."

"Every girl has a tag with her name on it on a hook on the Buddy Board," says Molly, showing me. "When you go in the lake, you flip your tag from red to green, and when you get out of the lake, you flip your tag to red again. That way, the counselors always know who's in the lake and who's out. Every girl has a buddy, and buddies hang their tags from the same hook because they always swim together. Margaret, you be my buddy. Flip your tag to green and put it on the hook with mine. Linda, you be Bobbie's buddy."

"Okay," says Linda. She leads Bobbie over to the Buddy Board and shows her how to flip their tags to green and hang them together on a hook.

It's really great how kind Molly and Linda and all the old campers are to the new campers like Bobbie and me. They're so nice about showing us what to do.

✪ ***Turn to page 41.***

"Why," puffs Linda, collapsing when we stop for lunch, "is every hike always uphill?"

"Uphill's where the views are," says Molly. She helps Linda slip her rucksack off her shoulders and puts it on the ground by her own and mine next to a tree stump. "The three of us can use this stump as a lunch table," she says.

When everyone is settled with sandwiches, I say, "On hikes, I'm always hurrying to keep up with Gem."

"Gem's an odd name," says Linda.

"It's really GM, for grandmother," I explain. "I slurred GM into Gem."

"Have you always lived at the ranger station?" asks Molly, who's perched on a rock next to me.

"Yup," I say. "The station's a log cabin in a little clearing in the forest. My parents lived there, too. They died when I was young."

"Oh, Margaret, I'm so sorry!" Molly exclaims.

"That must be hard," says Linda.

I nod. My heart always hurts when I talk about Mom and Dad. "Since then it's been just Gem and me." I pause, and then add, "Well, now there's Mischa. He's Gem's helper, just for the summer. He calls me

Margaret Jo, which is *not* my name. I don't like it!"

Molly laughs. "Did you hear my dad call me olly Molly? He's called me that forever!"

"Well, he's your *dad*," I say. "Mischa's just annoying with that Margaret Jo nonsense."

"Mischa is a Russian name," says Linda. "You must be grateful Mischa has come to help your grandmother the way our Russian allies are helping us win the war."

"I suppose I *should* be grateful," I say. "It's just that things have been all mixed up since he arrived. Gem and Bea and I used to do *everything* in the preserve together. Now Mischa is doing the things I used to do, like caring for injured animals. He's taking over, and I don't know what *I'm* responsible for anymore."

Molly has been listening carefully. "I know just how you feel," she says. "Responsibilities have been all mixed up at my house, too, ever since Dad came home from the war. It's hard to know what I'm supposed to do. I don't want to hurt Dad's feelings, but . . ." Her voice trails off.

✪ ***Turn to page 43.***

"Buddies have to stick together," says Molly as she and Linda and Bobbie and I walk out onto the dock. "Every once in a while, Miss Archer blows her whistle and buddies have to hold hands and raise them up for the counselors to see so they're sure everyone's safe."

Linda grabs Bobbie's hand now. "Come on, buddy Bobbie," she says. "BOMBS AWAY!"

Linda and Bobbie make a huge splash as they jump off the dock into the water. They remind me of Bea and me when they come up laughing, shrieking, and sputtering and then swim off in a race, kicking up a tsunami with their legs. I take Molly's hand so that we can jump off the dock together, too. But Molly wiggles her hand out of mine, sits on the dock, and gingerly lowers herself into the shoulder-high water.

That's odd, I think as I jump in. I swim out to the diving platform and climb the ladder. Facing Molly, I stand on my toes, raise my arms up, bounce, and dive, *s-l-o-o-p,* slicing cleanly into the water. I swim underwater, bob up for air, then go back under until I'm nearly back at the dock. Molly's still standing in the same spot, hugging herself. Her face looks vulnerable without her glasses, and her expression is self-conscious and a little unhappy.

What's wrong? I wonder. I'd like to be able to help Molly, but I don't want to be nosy. Should I just dive in and ask what's wrong, or should I be quiet and wait for her to say something?

✪ ***To ask Molly what's wrong, turn to page 47.***

✪ ***To wait for Molly to say something, turn to page 44.***

Molly looks worried. I think about her conversation with her dad. There was a moment then when she looked this same way. Something is bugging Molly. But before I can ask her about it, Barbara announces that lunch is over. "Time to get back on the trail."

We clean up and heave our rucksacks on our backs. Judy does a camper count. "All present and accounted for," she announces. "Let's move out!"

Once we're walking, Molly says, "I'm sorry about Mischa. But your life at the ranger station kind of sounds like living at camp all year round."

"I guess it sort of is," I agree. Molly and the other campers only get two weeks to enjoy what I have all the time. The hikers start to sing really loudly. I grin at Molly and say, "But at home the forest is quiet."

Molly laughs. "That is the great thing about camp. Lots of noisy new friends."

That makes me think about music camp. It might be fun to spend two months with a bunch of noisy new friends who love music.

Turn to page 45.

I don't like it when people push me, so I decide to keep quiet and wait for Molly to speak up.

I don't have to wait long. As soon as I swim over to Molly, she says, "I'm afraid to put my head underwater."

"Oh," I say. "I see." Now I understand why Molly wasn't too eager to join the swim meet.

"Last summer, I slipped off the dock and nearly drowned," says Molly. "I've been scared of being underwater ever since."

"No wonder," I say.

"Listen," says Molly earnestly. "I watched you dive and swim underwater just now. You're really good! I was wondering: Do you think you could help me?"

"Sure!" I say. "I'd be happy to—as happy as a clam!"

Turn to page 51.

45

It's late afternoon before we stop in a clearing under tall pine trees. An old rattletrap truck from camp meets us and we unload tents—which weigh a ton—for the girls who don't want to sleep out under the stars. The truck is also like an old-fashioned chuck wagon because the driver unloads food for our dinner. We all help Barbara and Judy build a campfire, and we cook hot dogs on sticks.

"Aren't you glad dinner is *not* 'great green gobs of greasy grimy gopher guts?'" jokes Judy.

"Yes!" everyone agrees.

I put baked beans in my bun, and then a hot dog, like I always do. Linda says, "Look! Margaret invented something new."

"My friend *Bea* invented this," I tell them. "We call it Bea's Beandog."

A few of the other girls try the beandog, including Molly. She grins after she takes a bite. "I like it," she says.

We all eat about twenty hot dogs apiece. That's something that's definitely the same in 1945: Hikers get hungry! Between the beans, and the ketchup and mustard and relish, all our hot dogs are dripping and messy. Soon we're all dripping and messy, too. I'm glad when we head off to the stream to wash up.

✪ *Turn to page 49.*

I decide to take the plunge and speak up, sink or swim.

I swim over to Molly and lean against the dock. "Are you okay, Molly?" I ask gently.

"I don't like to put my head underwater," Molly admits shyly. "I'm afraid."

"How come?" I ask.

Molly takes a deep breath. "Last summer, I slipped off this dock and nearly drowned," she says. She shudders, remembering. "It was so scary, the way the water sucked me down and closed over my head. I couldn't see or breathe or move. The counselors had to rescue me. Ever since then, I only put my head underwater when I absolutely *have* to. I'll be a Pollywog forever."

"What happened to you was awful," I say. "I don't blame you for being scared."

Molly smiles, and her shoulders relax a bit.

"If you want, I could help you. We *are* buddies," I say, nodding to the Buddy Board at the edge of the water.

"That would be great!" says Molly.

"Good," I say. "We can start right now. Ready to dive in?"

"Well, maybe not *dive in,*" says Molly.

I laugh along with Molly. "Fair enough," I say. "We'll go slowly, and we can stop whenever you need a break."

✪ ***Turn to page 51.***

After dinner, while we wash our sticky hands and faces in the stream. Linda says, "Hiking sure does make you hungry."

"Better hope the fish aren't hungry," jokes Molly, "or they'll nibble your fingers, thinking they're worms."

"Speaking of fish," says Linda, drying her hands on the seat of her shorts. "Have you decided, Molly? Are you going on that fishing trip with your father?"

Molly's smile fades. "I don't know," she says, tossing a pebble into the stream. She turns to me. "That's why things are tense between my dad and me right now," she explains. "I can't decide whether to go or not."

I smile at her sympathetically. "I know how hard it is to make decisions," I say.

"I think mine's impossible," says Molly. "When my dad was my age, he used to go fishing with *his* dad. Now he really, really wants me to go fishing with him. We'd get up before sunrise, go to a secret fishing spot, and stop for ice cream on the way home."

"That sounds like fun," I say. "Why don't you want to go?"

"I do want to go," Molly says. "But my dad has to travel most of this summer for his job. He's working in hospitals all over the state. Because of his schedule, there's only one day that will work. It's the same day as the orientation meeting for the school band. If I miss the meeting, I can't be in the band. I really, really want to be in band with Linda." Molly pauses and takes a deep breath. "If I go on the fishing trip, I'll miss out on band all year. Linda would be disappointed. And I'd be disappointed, too. But if I don't go on the fishing trip, my dad will be disappointed. And I hate the thought of disappointing him. So . . ." She shrugs and trails off.

"So no matter what you decide, you disappoint somebody," I finish for her. "Boy, I know how *that* feels! I've been offered a scholarship to music camp, and Gem thinks I should go. But my friend Bea doesn't want me to. No matter what I decide to do, I'll let somebody down."

"We're both stuck," says Molly.

She sounds miserable, so it's weird that Linda starts chuckling. Hasn't she been listening to us at all?

✪ ***Turn to page 54.***

I can tell Molly is nervous, so I say, "We don't have to start today. There's no rush."

"That's the thing," says Molly. "There sort of *is* a rush."

"You mean because of the swim meet on All Wet Day?" I ask.

"No, Miss Butternut said even Pollywogs can swim in the meet," says Molly. "I have another reason why I want to get over my fear, and I've only got these two weeks at camp to do it."

"Why?" I ask. "What is it?"

"Well," says Molly. "As soon as I get home from camp, my dad wants us to go on a fishing trip together. It's a tradition he and his dad had to mark the end of summer, and now Dad wants to start the tradition with me. Part of the tradition is that whoever catches the first fish celebrates by jumping out of the boat into the lake."

"And maybe *you'll* catch the first fish," I say, understanding Molly's dilemma. "Does your dad know that you're too scared to jump in and swim underwater?"

Molly nods, and I think of her dad's comment: "Look out for one another—especially in the water."

"I don't want him to think I'm a baby about it," says Molly. "I'd love to surprise him by showing him I've gotten over my fear." She looks resolute. "Our soldiers fighting in the war have to be brave. I have to be brave, too."

"For your dad?" I ask.

"*Especially* for my dad," says Molly. "He was away at the war for three years. I want him to be proud of how I've changed while he was away."

I try to reassure her. "Molly, I only just met your dad, but I can tell that he is proud of you."

She sighs. "He might be disappointed in me if we go on the fishing trip and I'm a big chicken." Molly looks pretty miserable at the possibility.

"I know how it feels to be afraid of disappointing people you love," I say. "I have to make a decision about going to a music camp. If I go, I'll disappoint my best friend, Bea. If I don't go, I'll disappoint my grandmother." I sigh. "I don't like making choices unless I *have* to."

"And I don't like swimming underwater unless I *have* to," Molly says ruefully. "I guess we're both sunk."

"No," I say firmly. "*You* are *not* sunk. I am going to

teach you to swim underwater."

"Well, then *I* am going to help *you* make decisions," Molly says just as firmly. "Start by being honest. Say what's on your mind."

I laugh. "Okay. Swimming's on my mind. Let's get started!"

Molly laughs, too. "Okay," she says. "Good decision. What do I do?"

Then it hits me. I've never taught anyone to swim before. I'm not sure I've ever taught anybody to do *anything* before.

✪ ***Turn to page 56.***

✪ 54 ✪

"What's so funny?" Molly asks Linda.

"Oh," says Linda. "I was just thinking about worms."

"Worms?" Molly asks.

"Yes, and how I hate them," says Linda, "and how last summer you and I were on opposing Color War teams. I was on the Red Team and you were on the Blue Team. I got so serious about my team winning the war that I betrayed you, and then you threw worms on me. Remember?"

Linda looks sideways at Molly, and when Molly meets her eyes they both laugh. "I remember!" says Molly. "It seemed like the right thing to do for my Blue Team. You and I were bitter enemies during Color War."

"You guys seem to have forgiven each other," I say.

"That's what friends do," says Molly.

"Exactly," says Linda sincerely. She playfully socks Molly's shoulder.

"Are you saying that whomever Margaret and I disappoint will forgive us because they love us?" Molly asks.

Linda nods. "Eventually," she says.

"Well," Molly says. "I still don't know whether I'll choose to go on the fishing trip or not. But now all I can think about is *worms*."

We laugh, but a wiggly thought has wormed its way into my mind: Linda says friends forgive one another. Will Bea forgive me? I want to find out.

Should I go home now? Or should I stay for the campout?

✪ ***To go home, turn to page 62.***

✪ ***To stay for the campout, turn to page 59.***

I think fast. I didn't learn to play the flute all at once. I took it one step at a time. That's what I'll do with Molly.

"Okay," I say to Molly. "Step One, get your hands wet, and then pat your face all over."

"This is easy," says Molly as she wets her face with lake water.

"You're ready for Step Two," I say. "Bend your knees so the water touches the bottom of your chin."

Molly bobs down and pops up. She has a beard of water drops dripping off her chin.

"Step Three," I say.

But we can't move on to Step Three, because just then, Miss Archer blows her whistle. She shouts, "Early Out!"

Before I can ask what that means, Linda and Bobbie swim up.

"Hey, you two," says Linda, treading water. "Bobbie and I are going to do Early Out and go back to the cabin and get ready for inspection and flag lowering. Come on."

"Not just yet," Molly says to Linda. "Margaret and I had a heart-to-heart talk, and she's going to teach me to swim underwater. We've just begun."

"Well, that's good," says Linda. "Bobbie and I will stay and help."

"Uh, thanks but no thanks," says Molly. "I don't want an audience. You girls go ahead. We'll come later."

"Oh!" says Linda. She sounds a bit surprised. "Okay." Swiftly, she lifts herself out of the water onto the dock. "Let's go, Bobbie."

They leave, and I make up more steps. Molly and I are laughing and having so much fun that we're surprised when Miss Archer blows the whistle and shouts, "Everybody out." We're last in line to turn our Buddy Board tags, and by the time we get to Tent Ten, everyone else is already dressed.

"Hurry up, you two," Linda says to us as she helps Bobbie tie her blue neck scarf just so. "The counselors won't like it if we're late for inspection and the flag lowering ceremony."

Once again, Molly says to Linda and Bobbie, "You girls go ahead."

"No, *you* two hurry," says Linda, crisp and impatient. "Then we can all go together."

Should I listen to Linda and hurry? Or should I

follow Molly's lead and take my time?

My indecision must be written all over my face, because Molly says, "Okay, Margaret, you want to get better at making decisions, right? So here's your first lesson: Say the first thing that comes to your mind."

✪ ***To say, "I want to hurry," turn to page 60.***

✪ ***To say, "I need a bit more time," turn to page 65.***

I'm not ready to go home. I'm determined to try something new, to face what's unfamiliar and unknown. Also, I cannot bear to say good-bye to Molly and Linda yet. So I plunge my hands into the stream and splash my face and say nothing.

The night air is warm and soft, but even so, after washing off in the cold, clear stream, it feels good to crawl into our sleeping bags.

Just as we're drifting off to sleep around the campfire, Linda sits up. "What was that?" she gasps.

"What?" asks Molly, sitting up in her sleeping bag. "What was what?"

"That," says Linda as a stick snaps close by.

Shirley sits up. "I heard it too," she says.

Now I'm sitting up.

"Something's out there in the woods," Linda says. "And its coming toward us!"

Turn to page 64.

I want to hurry so we can all go together," I say. "Besides, I'm a quick-change artist. Come on, Molly. We can be ready in no time."

"That was a good first lesson," Molly says with a grin. "Now, I bet I can change faster than you can."

Linda and Bobbie laugh as Molly and I race to get out of our wet suits and into our dry clothes. When I'm dressed, I pat my shorts pocket to be sure my pin is safe.

"Got everything?" Linda asks, watching me.

"Yup!" I say. "Come on. Let's race. On your mark, get set, go!"

Molly, Linda, Bobbie, and I charge out of the tent and run all the way to the flagpole. I run as fast as I can, but Linda wins the race. We stand at attention, lined up facing the flagpole. I watch as everyone holds out their hands in front of them for inspection, and I do the same.

Miss Archer and Miss Butternut walk up and down the line of campers, looking at our hands, being sure our shirts are tucked into our shorts, adjusting some girls' neck scarves, and reminding other girls to straighten their caps.

Linda nudges me. "Stand up straight," she whispers. "You have to pass inspection if you want dinner. You're in the army now."

✪ ***Turn to page 75.***

"You know what, you guys?" I say. "I'm going back."

"Back to camp?" Molly asks.

I shake my head. "Back home. I want to talk to Bea about music camp."

"Now?" Molly asks. She sounds disappointed.

No-nonsense Linda says, "We'll miss you, but if you're ready to talk, then it's a good idea to go. The sooner you tell her what you've decided, the sooner she can begin to forgive you."

"And you'll forgive me for leaving, right?" I ask.

"*Eventually,*" say Molly and Linda together, smiling at me.

"Thanks," I say. "Thanks for everything. I'll never forget you two."

"We'll never forget you either, Margaret," says Molly.

We hug, and then before I can change my always-seesawing mind, I ask Barbara and Judy for permission to go back to camp in the chuck wagon truck.

As the truck jounces me away, I wave good-bye to Molly and Linda and the others. I'm going to miss them!

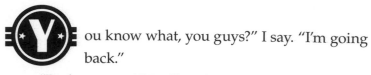

Back at camp, I rub the pin and *whoosh*! First darkness, then bright sunshine, and I'm back on the old wooden steps in the forest preserve behind our cabin. It's still midday. I look at my watch, and no time has passed since I first rubbed the pin.

I hurry through the pine-scented woods. As I head toward Bea's farm in the warm sunlight, I feel light and sunny, too. I'm eager to talk to Bea about the decision I've made. Music camp is for two months, but our friendship is forever. I know she'll understand and forgive me—as Molly and Linda would say—*eventually*.

✪ The End ✪

To read this story another way and see how different choices lead to a different ending, turn back to page 54.

"You know these woods are haunted, don't you?" says Dorinda from the other side of the campfire. She speaks in a low, hoarse whisper. "They're stalked by the ghost of Soggy Sam, who roams these woods in his soaking-wet clothes, looking for his lost love, Lorna, who drowned in the stream, on a night just like this. He'll sneak up behind you, and first you'll hear *drip, drip, drip,* and then you'll feel the touch of his icy finger on the back of your neck. *Brrrr!*"

And even though I know it's silly, I do feel tingling shivers running up my spine.

"You can hear him moaning, *Lorrrrr-naaaaa,*" Dorinda says. "Listen!"

And even though I know it's just the wind in the trees, I do hear moaning.

"You can hear his heavy footsteps coming closer, closer, closer . . . "

Just then, a log in the campfire breaks in two.

"*Eek,*" squeaks Linda.

"I'm scared," Shirley says. "I don't want Soggy Sam to get me!"

✪ ***Turn to page 68.***

65

I need a bit more time," I say honestly. "I'm sorry, Linda, but I'd hate to make you late."

"Oh, all right," says Linda. She sounds a bit disgruntled. "Come on, Bobbie."

And off she and Bobbie go.

"That was a good start at speaking your mind," says Molly as she tucks her shirt into her shorts.

After we change, we hang our wet suits on a clothesline strung between two trees behind the tent. "I know a shortcut to the flagpole," says Molly. "Follow me."

Molly's shortcut takes us behind the tennis court. We're bopping along, and then suddenly I stop and point to a bush heavy with berries and say, "Oh, look. Raspberries! We'll have to come back and pick some later."

I start to walk on, but Molly heads over to the bush and begins to fill her cap with berries.

"Aren't we going to be late?" I ask.

"No, the bugle hasn't blown yet," says Molly. "And even if we are late, it'll be worth it. Everyone is going to be *very* happy about this raspberry bush."

"Really?" I ask.

"Sure! I don't know about you," says Molly, "but I've hardly had any fresh berries since the war began."

"How come?" I ask. By now, Molly and I are on our knees picking the berries low to the ground. I'm filling my cap, too. We're both getting pretty sticky and our knees are grass-stained.

Molly looks at me as if I'm crazy. "Because of rationing, of course," she says. "We don't grow berries at home. Just a Victory garden with a bumper crop of turnips."

I'm not sure what a Victory garden is, or rationing, but Molly sure is excited about these raspberries.

"At least we don't have to ration hot water," Molly says. "I read that the English princesses—Margaret and her sister Elizabeth—have to ration bathwater. There's a black line around the bathtub in the palace, and they can't fill the tub above that line."

Rationing must mean limiting. And even princesses had to do it? "No kidding!" I say. "I thought princesses lived in luxury."

"Not during a war," Molly says, shaking her head. "Everyone in England—all over Europe, really—has been living without luxuries for a long time. They've had to sacrifice even more than we Americans have."

I had no idea.

Just then, the bugle begins to blow.

"Run!" says Molly.

✪ *Turn to page 70.*

Dorinda has made us *all* scared. Molly, Linda, and I scoot closer together. We lie on our backs and pull our sleeping bags up to our noses so that Soggy Sam can't finger our necks. I'm sure the other girls are like me, and can't help seeing shadows darker than the darkness slip between the trees, and can't help imagining that the stream sounds mournful as it rushes over the rocks, moaning, *"Lorrrr-naaaa."*

"If only we hadn't camped so near the stream," whispers Marie. "We've made it too easy for Soggy Sam to get us."

"Look! I'm Ssssoggy Ssssam," hisses Dorinda. She holds her flashlight under her chin and makes a gruesome face, moaning, *"Lorrrr-naaaa."*

"Aaaaahhh!" we all shriek, pulling our sleeping bags up over our heads.

"Dorinda," scolds Barbara. "That's enough. No more ghost stuff. Time to sleep."

For a while, there are no sounds but the swoosh of the stream, the crackle of the fire, and the restless wriggling of all of us shaky scaredy-cats inside our sleeping bags. Just as we're about to drift off to sleep, Dorinda wails one last muffled, *"Lorrr-naaa."*

"Now I'll *never* go to sleep," wails Linda. "I'm too scared."

"Me, too!" the rest of us whimper in agreement.

✪ ***Turn to page 72.***

We get to the flagpole just as the bugle call is ending, and we put our hats full of berries on the ground behind us. All the campers are standing at attention in two lines facing the flagpole. They're holding their hands out in front of them, palms up.

"Uh-oh," Molly grimaces, dusting dirt off her knees. "I forgot about inspection."

Sure enough, when Miss Butternut inspects us, she says, "Molly and Margaret, I think you've forgotten our Camp Gowonagin motto: 'Tidy and True.' Your shirts are untucked and dirty, your knees are grass-stained, and your hands aren't Camp Gowonagin clean! They're pink and sticky. Didn't you wash them?"

"Well," says Molly. She picks up her hat and shows it to Miss Butternut. "Margaret found a raspberry bush."

"Raspberries!" everyone shouts happily. The girls near me thump me on the back and say thank you. Someone calls out, "Three cheers for Margaret!" And everyone hollers, "Hip, hip, hooray! Hip, hip, hooray! Hip, hip, hooray!"

It's amazing how excited they are about fresh berries. Rationing must have been a big sacrifice.

After the cheer, Miss Butternut laughs. "A raspberry bush is good news," she jokes. "*Berry* good news." She pops a raspberry into her mouth. "Delicious! Molly and Margaret, I'll let your messiness go this time, because I'm glad about the berries. But I expect you to look shipshape-sharp for inspection tomorrow, and *do* wash your hands before dinner tonight." She turns to all the campers. "What's our Camp Gowonagin motto, girls?"

"Tidy and True!" we all shout together.

✪ ***Turn to page 75.***

But eventually, I guess we do sleep, because next thing I know, the sun is shining and I smell a campfire, and—

"Bacon!" says Linda. "I've hardly had bacon since the war started."

"It's a special treat," Barbara agrees.

In fact, all the campers seem really, *really* happy about the bacon.

Molly says, "The end of the war will mean the end of rationing." She savors a bite of bacon. "I can't wait to get rid of our ration cards and go shopping and buy whatever we want!"

Everyone agrees, and Judy says, "It's patriotic to eat less meat and sugar and butter. The soldiers need that food. You should all be proud of what you've done to help the war effort."

I eat my bacon and feel kind of guilty. I've never had to go without a certain kind of food because someone else needed it.

Breakfast helps everyone feel less groggy and cranky after our fretful night's sleep. Although the day is gray and gloomy, with a heavy sky that threatens rain, everyone is cheerful and energetic as we pack up.

"Come on, campers," says Barbara with cheerful enthusiasm. "Forward, march!"

"What's the first rule of hiking?" Judy asks us.

"Stick together!" we shout in reply.

When we set off hiking, we sing the "gopher guts" song really loud, and after that, the girls teach me lots of Camp Gowonagin songs. We sing and laugh and talk nonstop. In fact, I'm out of breath when we stop for a rest in a wide clearing. But Kathy has so much energy that she demonstrates how to do backward somersaults.

"Watch!" she says. She squats, falls back, and rolls. "Ta-da!" she cheers when she's sitting upright again. "I hug my knees tight under my chin," she explains. "That's the trick."

"Look!" says Molly, not to be outdone. "I can do a cartwheel." *Floop!* Molly spins, feet-over-head-over-heels, quick and easy, and then she says to me, "You do one, too, Margaret."

I make a dubious face. "I've never been able to do a cartwheel before," I say. But then, I've never been transported back to a girls' camp in 1945 before either! Isn't this adventure all about trying new things? So, doing a cartwheel—should I give it a whirl?

✪ *Turn to page 77.*

We all put our hands over our hearts as two counselors lower the flag and we sing the Camp Gowonagin song:

God bless Gowonagin!
Camp that we love!
Raise the flag high,
Never say die,
While the red, white, and blue flies above!

Standing next to Molly as the flag is lowered, I can tell that everyone loves camp, just as the words of the song say. Even though I've only been here for a few hours, I like it a lot, too. Everyone seems so happy to be here and proud of what they're doing. *Would music camp be like this?* I wonder.

We head to the Dining Hall next, where we go through a line to get our dinner. I'm always ready to eat after swimming, but today I'm especially hungry. The meat loaf, mashed potatoes, and green beans look delicious.

"All the vegetables we eat are from the camp's Victory garden," Molly tells me as I get a big scoop of beans. "We don't use any canned vegetables. The soldiers need them more." Molly sounds very proud.

After dinner, everyone heads to the lake. As darkness falls, the counselors build a fire on the shore, and we sit around it in a circle, our faces lit by firelight. Sparks fly up into the sky. We sing rounds, like "Row, Row, Row Your Boat," and manage to get all confused, which makes me laugh until my stomach aches. Or maybe it's the five toasted marshmallows I eat that does that! Miss Archer tells a ghost story, and we all squash closer to one another, happily scared. I feel as if Molly and all the girls at Camp Gowonagin have been my friends forever.

Turn to page 79.

Okay," I say. "Here goes nothing." I stand, raise my arms above my head, and then hurl myself forward onto my hands. *Ouch!* I land on my bottom with a thud. "My cartwheel's a dud," I say, red-faced and embarrassed.

"No, it looked pretty good," says Molly reassuringly.

"You should have seen mine when I first learned," jokes Kathy. "It was a disaster."

"Try again, Margaret," Patty urges.

I hesitate, but then all the girls cheer for me:

Gowonagin! Gowonagin!
Go on again and try!
You can win! You can win!
Go on again and try!

So I swat the pine needles off my hands and the seat of my shorts and get ready to try again.

"Wait," says Molly. "This time I'll help."

She stands next to me and catches my feet and guides them up and over and down. *Clonk!* I still land like a ton of bricks, but at least I land on my feet.

"Hooray!" cheer all the campers.

"That's the way, Margaret," claps Barbara.

Judy says, "That's showing 'em the old Camp Gowonagin spirit!"

I blush and grin. My cartwheel is not going to win me any Olympic gold medals in gymnastics. It's far from perfect, but it's better than it was, thanks to Molly's help. I'm glad I took a chance in front of my new friends. I tuck that idea away, just in case I decide to go to music camp, where I hope to make many more new friends.

The rest of the group packs up to move on, and Judy does a camper count. Before we put our rucksacks on, I say, "Hey, Molly and Linda, let's all do cartwheels at the same time."

"Okay!" say Molly and Linda.

Linda says, "On your mark, get set, go!"

✪ *Turn to page 81.*

Later, when we're in our bunk beds in Tent Ten, I put my pin underneath my pillow to keep it safe. Then the bugler plays "Taps," and everyone sings softly:

Day is done.
Gone the sun,
From the lake, from the hills, from the sky.
All is well. Safely rest. God is nigh.

"G'night!" everyone says to one another as they cozy down into their bunks.

"G'night, girls!" says Betty. She unhooks the lantern that hangs in the middle of the tent. "I'm going to a meeting with the other counselors-in-training. I'll be back soon. Sleep well."

Whoa, it's dark in the tent without that lantern! I pull my blanket up to my chin. Then the weirdest thing begins to happen. My throat aches, and I don't feel that "all is well," or that I can "safely rest."

Maybe it's the funny, familiar sounds of twanging bullfrogs and chirping crickets that make me long for home. Or maybe it's the sweet swish of the wind riffling the trees the way it does in the forest preserve or the way the moon shines silver and bright just as it does through my window at home. I can't help it. I sniffle.

"What's the matter?" asks Linda, whose bunk is next to mine. She flicks on her flashlight and shines it on me.

I sniffle again.

The top half of Molly suddenly appears. She's hanging upside down from her bunk above mine, her long braids dangling. "Are you homesick?" she asks.

✪ ***To say you're not homesick, turn to page 82.***

✪ ***To say you are homesick, turn to page 84.***

But as I fling myself upside down, I hear a soft *plunk*. Oh no! The pin has dropped out of my pocket! I get on my knees and frantically scrabble through the leaves and pine needles. I've got to find that pin or I'll never be able to go home.

"What are you looking for?" Linda asks as the rest of the group starts walking. She and Molly are hanging back.

"A pin," I say. "It fell out of my pocket."

"I'll help you find it," says Molly.

"No!" I say sharply. I'm afraid that if someone else rubs the pin—or even *touches* it—she'll disappear. "I mean, no thank you. You guys go ahead. Stay with the group. I'll catch up."

Molly shakes her head. "We have to stick together."

"We'll wait," says Linda, sitting on a tree stump.

"Okay, but let me search for it myself," I insist.

Linda shrugs, and Molly says, "Sure."

"Is your pin valuable?" Linda asks.

You have no idea! I think.

Turn to page 83.

I do miss home, but I know I'll be okay here, with my new friends. I want to stay, and that means being brave like the soldiers Molly was talking about.

I shake my head no at Molly, and say, "I'm fine." Then I roll over. I take a deep breath. I think about how nice Molly and Linda—everyone at Camp Gowonagin—has been. I grin. *You know what?* I think. *I* am *fine.*

Turn to page 100.

Quickly, I sift handfuls of pine needles, lift leaves, and run my hands over the damp ground and gnarled tree roots. I've been searching only a moment or two—even so, I'm about to burst into frustrated tears—when my hand feels a bump in a little crevice under a rock. It's the pin! Now I have to fight back tears of relief. "I found it!" I cry, holding it up.

"Good!" say Molly and Linda, thumping me on the back.

My heart is still beating hard and my hands are shaky as I secure the pin to the inside of my shorts pocket. *I'll never be so careless about this pin again,* I think. I shiver to think of what would happen if I had lost it.

Turn to page 87.

At the lake, Molly told me, "Speak your mind," and that gives me a newfound courage to say what I am feeling. I take a deep breath. "I've never spent the night away from home, except for sleepovers at Bea's house," I admit. "Sorry to be such a baby." I wonder: *Would I be this homesick at music camp?*

"Everybody gets homesick at some point at camp," says Molly.

"Really?" I ask. "Even you two?"

Linda nods. "You happen to be talking to the official Camp Gowonagin Homesickness Team. We're the world champions of homesickness."

"Two of the all-time greats," adds Molly. "At first, we didn't admit it to anyone, not even each other. But when we did admit it, we cried and cried."

"How'd you get over it?" I ask.

"We told each other to think of the soldiers fighting in the war," says Molly, "and how brave they have to be when they are in such danger and so far away from home."

Home. I really want to go! Do I have the nerve to say so straight out, even though it will disappoint Molly and Linda? Thanks to Molly, I do.

"I think . . . I think I want to go home," I say to Molly and Linda.

"Well, okay," says Molly. "Yes, if you want to, you should. But don't go tonight. Maybe after breakfast tomorrow."

"Breakfast is really good here," says Linda. "It's usually pancakes with lots of maple syrup. Maple syrup isn't rationed, so you can really pour it on."

"And I hope you'll stay for Morning Swim," says Molly. "So we can keep going with my swimming lessons."

"Right," says Linda. "Your swimming lessons for Molly are *dolphinately* an important *porpoise* for staying."

"Oh, Linda," moans Molly. "*Clam up.*"

Now they've got me giggling. I swipe my tears off my cheeks. "Is this how you talked each other out of being homesick last summer?" I ask.. "By telling terrible puns?"

"Noooo," says Linda. By the light of her flashlight, I see her exchange a look with Molly, who nods as if in answer to a silent question. Linda goes on. "Our counselor showed us something so wonderful it made us forget all about being homesick," she says. "It made us want to stay at camp."

"Oooh, what?" I ask, alert with curiosity.

"Come on," says Molly, silently swinging down from her bunk. "Come see."

✪ ***Turn to page 89.***

We shoulder our rucksacks and set forth on the trail. We've only gone a few hundred feet when the trail takes a sharp turn and forks. One path leads uphill, and the other path goes downhill.

"Uh-oh!" says Linda, anxiously. "Which way did the rest of our group go?"

"We fell so far behind that I can't see or hear them," says Molly. "This is terrible."

"It's my fault," I say apologetically. "If you hadn't waited for me to find my pin, we wouldn't be separated from the others."

"But we'd be separated from you," Molly says. "The three of us have to stick together."

"Which path should we follow?" wails Linda.

As usual when faced with a quandary, I hesitate. "Which way is the pond, do you think?" I ask.

At the very same moment, Molly says, "Uphill," and Linda says, "Downhill."

Just then, the skies open up and rain starts to fall, *hard*.

"Oh *no*," Linda groans. "*Now* what'll we do?"

"We've been headed uphill the whole time," says Molly, "ever since we left camp yesterday." She speaks confidently, "So I say we should go uphill."

"But we're going to a pond," says Linda, logical as always, "and ponds are usually downhill, right?"

Molly turns to me. "Margaret, *you* decide."

I square my shoulders. This is no time to have an attack of the Margaret Maybes. I've spent enough time hiking in the woods to know that we're in trouble. It's dangerous to hike in the rain, and it's even more dangerous to be separated from your group. We can't waste time. We've got to catch up with the others as quickly as possible. I've got to make a smart, safe decision, and *fast*.

✪ ***To decide to go uphill,***
***go online to* beforever.com/endings.**

✪ ***To decide to go downhill,***
turn to page 91.

89

Moving as quietly as possible, we slip our sockless feet into our shoes and tiptoe out of the tent. I'm shivery in my lost-and-found pajamas because I'm excited, and it's hard not to be seized by a fit of nervous giggles. Molly and Linda lead me up a hill behind the Dining Hall on a path lit by moonlight. On the other side of the hill, the land flattens a bit, and I see fields that touch the horizon.

"What are we—?" I begin.

"Shh," shushes Molly. She and Linda stand on the lowest rung of the split-rail fence that borders the field. Molly gestures to me to stand next to her.

"Just wait," says Linda.

I see graceful, drifting shadows first, cast by the moonlight.

Then, "Horses!" Linda whispers joyfully.

Of course I've seen horses in pastures on Bea's farm, but these horses look magical running across the field, their coats made shiny by the moon.

We gaze at the horses for several silent minutes. Then I see something that makes me catch my breath. There, next to its mother, is a foal a few weeks older than Aurora's foal. The foal trots across the field and casts its moon shadow on the grass. *Moon Shadow.* Suddenly, I miss Bea so much it hurts.

✪ ***Turn to page 93.***

I say, "Water runs downhill, so that's probably where the pond will be. Let's follow Linda's idea."

Hiking downhill on a rain-slicked path is tough. It's hard to keep our footing on the slippery pine needles. Soon we are polka-dotted with spatters of mud and our saddle shoes squish with every step. It isn't raining anymore, but discouraging drips drop on us from every tree branch. Our shirts are drenched and our spirits are sinking, going downhill as fast as the path is. No one says anything, but I'm pretty sure we're all thinking that this was a mistake.

Linda is leading the way and I'm right behind her. I see her slide, grab wildly for a tree branch, and land on her bottom, *thud*! "Oof!" she exclaims, suddenly sitting in a mud puddle.

"Oh, *Linda*," groans Molly.

But Linda grins. She scoops up handfuls of mud and lets it drizzle down. To the tune of the "gopher guts" song, Linda sings, *"Big brown blobs of slurpy, murky, mucky mud."*

Linda looks so mud-freckled and funny that we all have to laugh. We help Linda stand up, and I pour water from my canteen over her hands to rinse off the mud. We all laugh again when Linda unthinkingly tries to dry her hands on the seat of her shorts—which are covered with mud, of course!

Laughing lightens our feet and our moods, and after Linda's mudslide, we all cheer up. The sky lightens a bit, too, and a sluggish breeze tries to blow the stubborn gray clouds away. After we've walked another half hour or so, Molly stops short and whispers, *"Shh!"*

"What?" asks Linda in a hiss.

Molly doesn't answer. She frowns and holds her finger up to her lips to signal quiet. She tilts her head, and we listen hard. We all hear it at the same time: bushes rustling, sticks cracking under someone's—or some*thing's*—foot, even soft whimpering. We clutch one another, quaking in fear, and look into the undergrowth expecting to see Soggy Sam lumber toward us threateningly.

✪ ***Turn to page 94.***

I love horses," murmurs Linda. "Even though I don't know how to ride. In fact, before last summer, I'd never even *seen* a real horse before. When our counselors brought us here, it was so exciting."

"Bringing homesick campers here is a secret Camp Gowonagin tradition," says Molly. "Now you're part of that tradition, Margaret. Congratulations."

"Thanks," I say, thinking of Bea and our tradition of swimming every day during the summer.

Molly says, "And thanks to Margaret, I *may* even be brave enough for Dad's tradition of jumping out of the boat on our fishing trip."

"So, Margaret," asks Linda, "has the tradition of seeing these horses helped you decide to stay at camp?"

I'm torn. Seeing the horses has made me yearn to be with Bea and Moon Shadow. But I sure do like being with Molly and Linda, too.

To go home,
turn to page 99.

To stay,
turn to page 95.

We wait, but nothing comes out of the thicket of bushes. Molly separates herself from our huddle. "I'm going to go see what's in there," she says bravely.

"We'll all go," says Linda, just as bravely. "We stick together, remember?"

Molly steps forward, stoops, lifts a low-hanging branch, and ducks into the thicket. She takes a few steps before she stops suddenly. Underneath a tangle of bushes we see—

"A dog!" says Molly. "Oh, he's so cute!"

Linda says, "I think he's hurt."

"It looks like he's stuck," I say. The dog is whimpering and scrabbling to move, but his collar is caught on something. I take off my bulky rucksack and lie on my stomach on the ground. I stretch my arm and try to reach him.

"Don't touch him!" warns Linda. "He may bite."

I can't reach him, but I know I have to do something to help this poor dog. I think of Gem and how she helps injured animals.

✪ ***Turn to page 96.***

I grin at my two new friends who have been so kind to me. "I'm part of the Camp Gowonagin Homesickness Team now," I say. "And I'm in on the secret traditional cure for homesickness, too. I'm proof that it works! I can't wait to see what other traditions there are."

"You mean you'll stay?" asks Linda, who likes to be definite. "You'll be in the swim meet on All Wet Day?"

"You bet," I say.

"And you'll keep on teaching me to swim underwater?" asks Molly.

"For sure!" I say. "Another lesson tomorrow."

"Good," says Linda. She yawns. "But we need some sleep before tomorrow is today. Let's go back to our tent before I fall asleep right here."

Cheerfully, we walk back to Tent Ten, casting our own moon shadows on the path ahead of us.

Turn to page 100.

"His collar is stuck on something," I say. "I need to get close enough to untangle him."

"We'll help you," Molly says, taking off her rucksack.

Linda hesitates for a moment, but then she does the same.

"I'll crawl under the bushes," I say.

"Okay," says Molly. "Linda and I will hold the branches up so they won't scratch you."

"Be careful," I say.

"You, too," says Molly.

I slither on my stomach, pulling myself forward with my arms. All the while, I'm saying softly, "Don't worry, pup. It's all right, it's all right."

The dog manages to wag his tail to show me he's not afraid, and that he's glad to see me. "Are you hurt?" I ask when I'm next to the dog. His collar *is* stuck on a branch. When I untangle him, I see that the dog has some scratches on his back and leg from trying to get himself free.

"Molly," I say. "My canteen is empty. Can you hand me yours?"

She does, and I pour water over the dog's wounds. The dog licks my hands as if to say thank you. Then he licks my face.

"The scratches aren't serious," I say. I crawl back out, and the dog follows me. Standing, I pick up the dog and turn to Molly. "The scratches on his leg are bleeding a little. Can you bind them with your camp tie?"

Molly does, and the dog licks *her* hand. "Oh you sweet dog!" she says. "Wow, Margaret, you knew exactly what to do."

Linda sounds impressed as she says, "You were right about him not biting."

"Gem taught me how to calm injured animals," I say. "And this little guy wouldn't hurt a flea."

Gently we pet the dog, who has been sniffing at the blue scarf around his leg. He's so happy that he wiggles all over with joy. "Shall we use my camp scarf as a leash and keep him with us?" asks Linda. "Maybe he'll lead us back to his home so we can telephone camp."

"But he doesn't belong to us," Molly says sadly. "Maybe we should let him go free so that he can find his own way home."

Molly and Linda turn to me. "You know more about animals, Margaret," Molly says. "What should we do?"

It's up to me to make the decision.

✪ *To let the dog go,*
turn to page 103.

✪ *To keep the dog with you,*
turn to page 107.

"Thank you for bringing me to see these horses," I say. "I love this Camp Gowonagin tradition. But I love my traditions with Bea, too. And remember how I told you that Bea's horse had a foal this morning? We named him Moon Shadow. And look—*this* foal has a moon shadow! It's time for me to go home. I don't want to miss a minute of watching *my* little Moon Shadow grow up."

"Sometimes my dad says that the worst thing about the war is that it robbed him of watching me and my brothers and sister grow up," Molly says. "Nothing can ever give our family back those years together that we missed when he was away."

"No wonder that he wants to spend as much time with you as he can," I say. "You know he'll love that fishing trip with you no matter whether you jump out of the boat or not, right?"

"I guess he will!" says Molly. "You're right."

"And you're right about going home," says Linda. "If I had a chance to spend time with a newborn foal, I'd take it."

Turn to page 105.

I make sure my pin is still safely under my pillow, and then I fall asleep and dream of horses—especially Aurora's foal, Moon Shadow.

The next morning, I dress in my Camp Gowonagin uniform. As I slip the pin into my pocket, I think about how glad I am that I stayed.

At breakfast, I take part in one of the most popular Camp Gowonagin traditions: a pancake-eating contest.

Molly, Bobbie, Nancy, Carolyn, and Edie quit after four, but Linda and I chow on.

"I should warn you, Margaret: I'm last year's champion," says Linda as she eats her fifth pancake.

"I should warn *you*," I say, as I eat my fifth, too. "At home, my grandmother and I have a tradition called Syrup Sundays so I've had years of practice eating pancakes and maple syrup."

After her fifth pancake, Linda groans. "Can we call it a tie?"

"Well, maybe," I say, hesitating as I reach for another pancake.

But Molly says, "Margaret! No *waffling*! Get it?"

And our other tent mates cheer for me.

Since these just happen to be the best pancakes I

have ever eaten, I have no trouble finishing my sixth.

Linda reaches for her sixth pancake, but she just can't do it. "I'll sink in the lake if I eat another bite," she says.

That puts me over the top for the win.

"Impressive, Margaret," says our junior counselor, Betty.

"Thanks," I say.

"You lose, Linda!" crows Molly. She raises my arm up as if I have won a prize fight. "Look, folks," she says. "Our new champion—Margaret!"

Linda frowns. It's only a pancake-eating contest, but I can tell that she doesn't like losing. Her frown deepens when Molly leads my tent mates in a cheer:

Margaret, Margaret, she's our man!
If she can't do it, no one can!
Hoo-rah, hoo-rah, hoo-rah!

Oh dear, I think. If I had known it would bother Linda so much, I never would have eaten six pancakes. Now my heart feels as heavy as my pancake-packed stomach. I never intended to jeopardize that wonderful spirit of togetherness that we all felt last night. But it's too late now.

✪ *Turn to page 109.*

"We should let him go," I say. "His injury won't slow him down, so he'll be able to find his way home."

Molly, Linda, and I stand up and reshoulder our rucksacks and canteens. "Good-bye, buddy," I say to the dog.

He looks at us, wags his tail, and then trots off into the woods. He favors his injured leg a bit, but even so, he soon disappears. Watching him go, I say a silent thank-you to Gem for teaching me how to care for animals. Then I turn to my friends. "Thank you for helping."

"You did it all," Molly says quickly.

I shake my head. "It was teamwork."

"Well, team," Linda says. "How are we going to get ourselves back to camp? I have no idea where we are."

"Me, either," Molly says. "I bet Barbara and Judy are worried."

Linda says, "Margaret, you've grown up in the woods. Have you ever been *lost* in the woods?"

"Yes," I confess. "Once. I was seven, and Gem and I went for a walk in the spring, before the trails had been cleared. She told me to stay close, but I wandered off."

"Oh, no," Molly says. "Were you scared?"

I nod. "I was lost for a couple of hours because I was trying to find my way back. I was just walking in circles. When Gem found me, she taught me the first lesson of getting *un*lost in the woods: Stop moving. That makes it easier for searchers to find you. So right now, we need to stay in one spot and let ourselves be found."

Linda and Molly nod. They both look nervous.

"We'll be okay," I tell them. "We're still on a marked path. It's not like we're deep in the woods—or stuck in a bush. "

But my friends don't look reassured. Oh dear. I think I've *scared* them!

✪ ***Turn to page 112.***

We go back to camp, and I wait for Molly and Linda to fall asleep. Then I write a note:

Good-bye, Molly and Linda! Thanks for being so nice. I'll never forget you. We'll always be buddies. Hey, Molly, you know how you tell me to speak my mind? Well, here goes: Linda's a great swimmer. She's part fish, remember? Linda can be your Buddy Board buddy now and help you learn how to swim underwater so you can jump out of the boat for your dad. I o-FISH-ally turn over my teaching job to Linda so that she can FIN-ish what you and I started.

Love until the ocean waves and the seas run dry,

Margaret

I tiptoe noiselessly out of the tent and rub the pin. After the sound of rushing wind, I'm plunged into darkness and then surrounded by sunshine. I'm sitting on the wooden steps in the woods where my adventure began. Before I head home to Gem, I walk the familiar and well-loved route to Bea's family's farm.

Bea is in the barn with Aurora and Moon Shadow. When Bea sees me, she says, "I'm sorry I didn't come over for waffles."

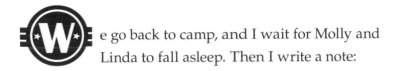

It takes me a moment to remember that the last time I saw Bea I was heading home for waffles. A lot has happened since then!

"That's okay," I say.

Bea grins. She says, "You missed Moon Shadow, didn't you?"

"I did," I say. "And I realized how much I'd miss you and our traditions if I went away to camp."

"I'd miss you, too," Bea says. "But I've been thinking about what Gem said. Eight weeks is not forever. Not when it's such a great chance for you to do something you love."

Wait—is Bea saying I should go to music camp? Has she changed her mind? And how about me? Molly said, "Speak your mind." Do I want to stay home, or do I want to go to music camp?

✪ ***To stay home,***
turn to page 114.

✪ ***To go to music camp,***
turn to page 124.

I don't think we should leave him alone," I say.

"Me, either!" say Linda and Molly. That's something we all agree on.

Linda takes off her neck scarf and we squat around the dog. But before we can slip the scarf around the dog's neck, he suddenly lifts his ears and barks, startling us. Molly, Linda, and I are so surprised that we fall back on our bottoms.

We look over our shoulders. Behind us we see a curly-haired teenage boy squatting with open arms. Joyfully, the boy calls out, "Maxie!" and just as joyfully, the dog scrambles to its feet, hobbles into the boy's arms, and licks his face so enthusiastically that the boy falls back on his bottom, too. The dog clearly knows and loves this boy!

"Danke! Danke schoen!" the boy calls to Molly, Linda, and me, between chin licks from the dog. *"Vielen Danke!"*

"That boy's speaking German!" Linda hisses. She jumps to her feet, drawing Molly and me up with her. *"He's* German."

Molly pulls in her breath, her eyes wide. I can see

from their faces that Molly and Linda are both scared stiff, but I'm not sure why.

"My dad told me there are prisoner of war camps in the U.S.," Molly says. "But I didn't know there was one near here."

"What?" asks Linda, horrified. "A prison camp? Here?"

"You think he's a *prisoner*?" I ask. "Why?"

"Look at the letters on his pants and shirt," Molly says. "P-O-W. That means 'prisoner of war.'"

Linda whispers in a tight, scared voice. "If he's out here in the woods," she says, "that makes him an *escaped* prisoner, right?"

"He's a German soldier?" I ask.

Linda nods. "Maybe he's a spy!" she says. "Maybe he'll hurt us!"

✪ ***Turn to page 116.***

All of us who chose to be in the swim meet are scheduled for Morning Swim right after arts and crafts, so we go back to our tent to pull on our suits. I have to wriggle into mine; quick-drying synthetic material hasn't been invented yet in 1945, so my suit is still damp from yesterday. Molly's quicker. Before the bugle blows, she's already left for the waterfront. I hurry to fold my shirt and my shorts and put them at the end of my bunk.

"What's that?" asks Linda as I take the gold pin out of my shorts pocket and slip it under my pillow.

"Oh!" I say. "Uh, nothing."

"It isn't *nothing*," says Linda tartly. "It's a *pin*."

How can I possibly explain about the pin and its powers?

Luckily, just then the bugle blows, so I don't have to answer Linda. She races off to the waterfront. I'm nervous that Linda saw me put the pin under my pillow, so I hastily slide the pin beneath my mattress instead. Then I run to the waterfront, too.

"Linda, you and Bobbie should be buddies again," Molly says briskly as soon as I arrive, breathless from running. "Margaret and I will buddy up again, too, so that we can pick up where we left off in my lessons."

"Oh. Okay," says Linda. Linda salutes Molly. "Yes, sir!" she barks. I can tell that Linda does *not* like being bossed by Molly.

After Molly and I flip our buddy tags, we walk out onto the dock. *Floop!* I dive off, swim underwater, then flip around and turn back to face Molly, who's sitting on the dock dangling her legs in the water.

"Can you teach me to dive like that?" Molly asks.

"Well, sure," I say. "Step by step. First, let's get you used to putting your head underwater. I think we're up to Step Thirteen, which is holding your nose and sinking down. Ready?"

Molly does Step Thirteen so well that we celebrate by having a tea party underwater. Molly holds the handle of her pretend teacup in one hand and daintily holds her nose with her other hand.

By the afternoon, she can be underwater without holding her nose at all. When the bugle blows marking the end of Afternoon Swim, most of the girls leave. But some choose to stay, including Molly and me. Molly practices staying underwater as long as she can. After that, I teach her to float on her back, which she does beautifully. "I really like this," Molly says happily. "It's like being on a cloud."

✪ *Turn to page 118.*

The second lesson is to not panic," I say, speaking to them softly, just as I spoke to the dog. "Let's find a shady spot to sit and wait so that anyone who is looking for us can see us easily."

We pick up our rucksacks and retrace our steps through the undergrowth to the trail. Linda spots a fallen log along the path, and we trudge over.

I sit down on the log and start to take a drink, but of course my canteen is empty. "How much water do you two have?" I ask my friends.

They both uncap their canteens and take turns pouring some of their water into my canteen.

"Thanks," I say.

Molly smiles. "At camp last year, we had classes in survival skills. Water is the most important thing to have when you're out in the woods."

"Right," Linda nods, opening her rucksack. "Food's pretty important, too. Look! I volunteered to carry some of the lunch supplies." Linda pulls out a small bag of cheese and bread. "We can make sandwiches!"

"Hooray," Molly says "Thanks, Linda!"

"You're welcome," says Linda. "I guess we'd better ration it to make it last."

"We'll be found before we need more than that to eat," I say quickly.

Linda looks doubtful. "I hope you're right," she says.

✪ *Turn to page 120.*

I grin at Bea. "I really want to stay home," I say. "We decided to raise Moon Shadow together this summer and I can't wait to begin. I want to watch him grow every day."

Bea hugs me. "I'm so glad," she says. She looks me in the eye and asks, "Do you think Gem will be disappointed in your decision?"

I think about Molly and her dad and how they both wanted each other to be happy. I know Gem and I feel that way about one another, too. I say to Bea, "Gem loves me. I'm pretty sure she'll understand." I cross my fingers on both hands. "Anyway, I hope so. I'm going home to find out—right now!"

"Okay, good luck," says Bea. "See you later."

As I come near our cabin, I see Gem working on her laptop at the picnic table. She looks up and says, "Hello, dear girl! I'm glad to see you. Can you help me? My laptop's not cooperating."

"Sure," I say. "I'm glad to help."

"Thanks," says Gem. As I fiddle with her laptop, Gem says, "What would I do without you?"

"Well," I say. "You'd be fine. But you're not going to have to do without me just yet. Not this summer anyway. I've decided to stay. I hope you're not disappointed."

"In you?" Gem asks. "Never."

I fling my arms around her and hug her with all my might.

✪ ***The End*** ✪

To read this story another way and see how different choices lead to a different ending, turn back to page 93.

Gently, the boy lifts the dog up in his arms and steps toward us. Molly and Linda take abrupt steps back. The boy snuggles his face in the dog's neck and then kisses the dog's ear. No one says anything for a long moment.

Then brave Molly says to the boy, *"Gesundheit."*

"What?" squeaks Linda.

"That's the only German I know," explains Molly.

"Howdy, pardner," says the boy.

"That's probably the only *English* that he knows," says Linda. "He probably learned it from cowboy movies."

The boy smiles and his brown eyes shine. He puts the dog down, points to it, and says, "Maxie." Maxie wags his tail cheerfully. The boy points to himself and says, "Johann."

Molly points to herself and says, "Molly." Then she points to us while saying our names: "Margaret and Linda."

"Molly!" Linda scolds. "Don't tell him our names." She is tense and wary.

"Tannenbaum!" I suddenly say to the boy. I turn to Molly and Linda. "That means Christmas tree," I say.

"I play that carol on my flute."

"Tannenbaum," nods the boy, pointing to a fir tree. Then he struggles to explain his situation. He pantomimes running. Then he taps his chest. He shades his eyes with his hand and looks all around anxiously, pantomiming searching. Then he hugs Maxie and says something in German.

"I think he's trying to tell us that he's been looking everywhere for his dog," says Molly to Linda and me. She turns to Johann. "Maxie's collar got caught on a bush, and he scratched his leg," she explains. She points to Maxie, makes a sad face, and whimpers. "We bandaged it." She points to the tie we wrapped around Maxie's leg.

"Ahh!" says Johann.

"Molly, keep talking," Linda whispers. "Margaret and I will circle from behind, and tackle him."

"What?" I ask, confused.

"He's an *enemy,*" says Linda, getting right to the heart of the matter. "We've got to capture him and take him back to Camp Gowonagin."

✪ ***Turn to page 122.***

For free choice after dinner, Linda and Bobbie go to the movie in the Recreation Hall, but Molly and I choose swimming so that Molly can have more practice. By the end of the evening, she can jump off the dock, sink under the water, and then bob up. I dive right next to her every single time to keep her company and encourage her.

"Look at my fingers," Molly says to Linda when we meet in Tent Ten before going to bed. "They're wrinkly, pink prunes."

"For a good *raisin,*" I pun.

"Well," says Linda, slipping into her pajamas. "You missed a great movie. It was a war movie with a mystery in it called *The Stolen Jewels.*" Linda looks at me out of the corner of her eye, which makes me uncomfortable. "The thief turned out to be someone that everybody trusted," she says. "She was a—"

But Molly talks over her. "Margaret is going to teach me to dive," she announces. "We're going to enter the diving competition at the swim meet."

"Diving?" asks Linda. "You?"

She sounds so skeptical that Molly tosses one braid over her shoulder and says, "Yes. Margaret is such a good teacher that I'm sure she'll have me diving very soon. I'll be leapfrogging out of the Pollywog Level in no time. Right, Margaret?"

"Ribbet," I say, nodding.

"You're both going to compete?" asks Linda.

"Yes," says Molly. "Margaret and me."

"Really?" says Linda. "*You* want to dive? You didn't even want to put your head underwater last summer."

"Last summer, Margaret wasn't here," says Molly, hugging me. "She's a great teacher." She grins. "She's a *whale* of a teacher."

Linda raises her eyebrows. "Evidently," she says. She flops onto her bunk and rolls onto her side, giving Molly and me the cold shoulder.

"What's eating her?" Molly silently mouths to me, tilting her head toward Linda.

I shrug, palms up.

✪ ***Turn to page 125.***

We haven't been separated from the others for that long," I explain calmly. "And Judy and Barbara are careful about doing camper counts. They probably already know we're missing. As soon as they walkie-talkie back to camp, the counselors will know we're missing, and they'll start looking for us."

"Do you think they'll find us before it gets dark?" Molly asks.

"I do," I say, glancing at my watch. "It's barely past noon."

"That's why I'm hungry," Linda says. "Who wants a sandwich?"

My stomach growls, and Molly and I say, "Me!" at the same time.

The bread's pretty squished, so the sandwiches don't look that good, but we all feel better after we've eaten.

"I hope that dog made it home and had some food," Molly says as she finishes her last bite. "I would have given him part of my sandwich."

"There are lots of farms around Camp Gowonagin," Linda says. "He probably doesn't live far away. He'll be home soon." I can tell she's trying to make Molly feel better about letting the dog go.

"I bet Linda's right," I chime in. "He looked healthy and well-fed, so I'm sure he wasn't gone from home long before he got stuck on the branch."

Molly's face brightens. "I guess it's a good thing we got lost so we could find him," she says cheerfully.

"Speaking of being found," Linda says, pointing up the trail. "Look." Molly and I turn, and I see two camp counselors walking down the hill toward us.

"Oh, hooray!" cheers Molly. "Betty and Miss Archer have found us!" She calls to them, "Ha-loo! Here we are!"

✪ ***Turn to page 127.***

"Gowonagin?" smiles the boy. He points down the hill. Then he points up the hill and pretends to march that way, giving us a little wave good-bye.

"I think he's trying to tell us that Camp Gowonagin is down there," I say. "And wherever he's going is up there."

Molly says, "We don't need to tackle him. He doesn't seem dangerous. I think he's going back to the prisoner of war camp with Maxie."

"I don't trust him," says Linda flatly. "We can't just let him go. Maybe he parachuted in and is on his way to Chicago or someplace to spy for the Germans. I saw a movie like that once. And if he is a runaway from a prisoner of war camp, we—"

"*Maxie* is the runaway," interrupts Molly. "All Johann did was come looking for his dog."

"Well, that still doesn't change the fact that Johann is a prisoner of war who is outside the camp," says Linda stubbornly. "He's not supposed to be wandering around the forest."

Molly and I look at each other. "Linda has a point," Molly says.

Linda says, "We *have* to stick with him to be sure he goes back to prison." She turns to Johann and points up the path. "Let's go," she says.

Johann clearly doesn't understand. He waves and says, *"Auf Wiedersehen,"* which obviously means good-bye. Johann whistles to Maxie, and they both start to walk up the path.

Linda shadows him, and reluctantly Molly and I follow close on her heels. We've only gone a few steps when Johann realizes that we're behind him.

He stops and points down the path. "Gowonagin *fur sie,"* he says, politely but firmly. It's easy to tell that he thinks we're mixed up. He waves and says, "So long, pardner."

Linda shakes her head at Johann. "Not 'so long,'" she says. "Lead on. We're going with you. We want to be sure you get back where you belong without disappearing into this forest of *tannenbaums."*

✪ ***Turn to page 129.***

"I don't want to leave you and Gem and Moon Shadow," I say. "But—"

Bea cuts me off. "I know."

"I'm sorry," I say. "But I'm going to go to music camp."

Bea holds up her hand to wave away my apology. "Margaret Maybe," she says with a crooked smile. "Listen to you. I'm proud of you. You made a decision!"

I smile, and suddenly we're hugging. Molly was right: It's good to speak your mind.

"I'll send you videos on your cell phone," Bea says. "That way you can still see Moon Shadow every day. I'll be sure you don't miss anything important."

"Thanks," I say. I grin. "But I'll still miss something very important. I'll miss *you*."

✪ The End ✪

To read this story another way and see how different choices lead to a different ending, turn back to page 22.

"Eek," shivers Molly the next morning as she's putting on her bathing suit. "My suit is cold and damp."

"It's *clammy,*" I joke.

"Which makes me feel *crabby,*" adds Molly.

"Har-dee har-har," says Linda. "That's so funny I forgot to laugh."

Molly swirls sharply. "Linda," she says. "Talk about crabby! Why are you mad at Margaret and me?"

"'Margaret and me, Margaret and me, Margaret and me,'" mimics Linda. "It's as if you've forgotten that I exist, Molly, except to boss me and tell me what to do. You and Margaret so are buddy-buddy that you exclude me. You two swim together, have heart-to-heart talks together, make plans together, and even make *puns* together, for Pete's sake. It's as if you wish I'd just disappear."

"Oh, Linda, no," I begin. "Molly doesn't—"

But Linda interrupts me. "You're just as bad, Margaret," she says hotly. "You waltz into camp and steal my best friend and stuff yourself with pancakes and shove me aside. Do you know how bad that feels?"

"I do," I say. "Ever since Mischa came, I've felt sort

of useless. He's robbed me of things Gem used to trust me to do, like taking care of the injured animals that she nurses back to health. So I *do* know how it feels to be left out, Linda. I'm sorry."

"It's too late for sorry now," says Linda. "I don't need to feel like a third wheel, and I don't need either of *you*." And with that, Linda yanks her bathing cap onto her head and storms off.

"Linda!" Molly calls after her. But it is no use. Linda ignores her.

✪ ***Turn to page 136.***

Molly, Linda, and I run to meet the counselors.

"Are you okay? Is anyone hurt?" asks the tall counselor.

"We're fine, Miss Archer," Molly says.

"Oh, thank goodness!" says Betty. Miss Archer uses the walkie-talkie to call camp.

"We have about an hour's walk to get back," Betty says. "How's your water supply?"

"Molly and Linda shared their water with me," I say. "We all have plenty."

Miss Archer is speaking into her walkie-talkie. "Roger that," she says. Then she clips it to her belt and puts her hands on her hips and shakes her head at Molly, Linda, and me. "You girls had us worried," she said. "I've radioed Barbara, so she and Judy and the other hikers know you are safe now. Come on. Let's get you back to camp. You must be tired and hungry."

"Linda had sandwiches for us," I say. "So we're actually okay."

Linda grins. "But about five more sandwiches would be okay, too," she says.

Betty takes off the rucksack on her back and reaches into it. "I have carrots," she says, holding out a bag of peeled carrots. "Would you like some?"

"Yes! Thank you," we all say as we each take one.

"Mmmm," Molly says after taking a big bite. "This is the best carrot I have ever eaten in my life! Thanks!"

I just nod and grin, agreeing with Molly. My mouth is too full of delicious carrot to speak.

✪ ***Turn to page 132.***

Johann looks puzzled. Again, he starts to go up the path, and again, when he sees us right behind him, he stops. He can't figure out why we're not taking the trail back to Camp Gowonagin.

It's Maxie who solves the go-stop-go problem. Now that he feels better, he's eager to be home. So, even though he has a limp, he moves pretty quickly up the path. Johann has no choice but to follow his dog. We tag along, dogging *him*.

Maxie leads us up one hilly slope and down another. Eventually, we come to a small pond. Across the pond and through the trees, we see a tall, chain-link fence, and inside the fence are buildings arranged in straight rows.

"Oh, my gosh," says Linda. "A prisoner of war camp, right *here*."

"It looks more like a *camp* than a *prison*," Molly says.

As we stare through the fence, Johann looks at us with confusion.

"*Now* what are we going to do?" asks Molly. "Do we tell someone that we found Johann in the woods? Or do we just let him sneak back in without being noticed?"

"If we tell someone he left camp, won't he get in trouble?" I ask.

"My dad says it's against army rules to be absent without leave," says Linda. "It's called being AWOL. Johann is AWOL. We have to tell someone."

"But he was just trying to find his *dog*," Molly insists. "And he *did* come back to camp on his own."

"For all we know, he had permission to leave!" I say hopefully.

"Huh, I doubt it," says Linda. "I think he's AWOL, and that means we need to report him. Otherwise *we* might get in trouble."

"What do you think we should do, Margaret?" Molly asks.

My mind is in a whirl. Johann was a soldier in the enemy army. Doesn't that make him partly responsible for all the awful things the German military has done? Should we treat him like an enemy? Would it be unpatriotic to help him? On the other hand, Molly's right: Johann doesn't seem dangerous. Right now, he's just a kid who wanted to find his dog. He didn't cause any trouble, and he didn't hurt us. Why shouldn't we let him go back to camp without being noticed?

Isn't that the *kind* thing to do? Isn't the war over?

✪ ***To alert the authorities,***
turn to page 134.

✪ ***To let Johann sneak back in,***
turn to page 138.

We're pretty tired, so the hike back to camp is quiet, without any boisterous rounds of the "gopher guts" song. We march single-file, with Miss Archer in front and Betty at the end of the line. The sun is strong and our wet clothes have dried, but they're crusty with mud. As the Camp Gowonagin flag comes into view, I see Molly tuck in her shirt, and Linda tries to brush off some of the mud. *It's not much use*, I think. *We're a mess.*

Miss Archer leads us past the Dining Hall to a square, squat building. The sign reads "Office." A woman with curly gray hair is waiting at the front door. "That's Miss Butternut, the camp director," Molly whispers.

"Leave your rucksacks here, girls, and come inside," Miss Butternut says. She sounds brisk and no-nonsense.

Linda and Molly and I exchange glances as we peel off our rucksacks. We follow Miss Butternut into a room with two large sofas facing each other. Miss Butternut, Miss Archer, and Betty sit on one, and Molly and Linda and I sit on the other.

"All right, campers. Barbara and Judy told me what

happened via walkie-talkie, and Miss Archer filled me in on where she found you. Now I'd like to know what you three have done and seen this morning."

Linda sits up straight and starts explaining—everything from the gymnastics that caused us to lag behind the group to our lunch by the log. Molly chimes in when Linda gets to the part about the dog, and she tells the counselors how much I know about animals and about staying safe in the woods. "Margaret told us to stay in one spot so you could find us," says Molly.

"Well, I couldn't have helped the dog without Molly's and Linda's help," I add quickly. "And they shared their water with me when I ran out. Besides," I say urgently. "It's *my* fault we got separated from the group—"

I stop short, remembering how frantically I looked for my pin. I knew I needed to find it myself because if Molly or Linda touched it, they might be transported to another time. And what about now? If I say something about the pin, will I have to show it to Miss Butternut? Will she take it from me?

✪ ***Turn to page 140.***

But I don't think it would be honest to let Johann sneak back into the camp. "He broke the rules by leaving," I say. "I think it's our responsibility to let the guards know he's officially back."

Molly sighs sadly. She says, "Sometimes the right thing to do is the hardest thing to do."

Linda and I nod in reluctant agreement.

"If we go with Johann, then we can explain what we know," I say. "Maybe he'll be in less trouble that way." Molly and Linda look slightly less miserable when I say that.

"We're coming with you all the way to the fence," Molly tells Johann. She points to herself, Linda, me, and Johann, makes a circle with her finger to show we're staying together, then points to the gate.

Now he nods in reluctant agreement, too.

We skirt the pond, staying hidden in the trees that encircle it, and follow the narrow, bumpy footpath that leads to a chain-link fence. On the other side of the fence, all the trees have been cleared away, and we see barracks arranged in arrow-straight rows. The sun glints on their metal roofs. Men dressed like Johann in prisoner of war uniforms move around the buildings, and other men dressed in army uniforms do, too.

Johann lifts Maxie up into his arms, holds the dog close to his chest, and looks at us. His face is calm. He doesn't look happy, but he doesn't look terrified, either. He doesn't bolt off and run away. He stands straight and still and waits to see what happens. Maxie, on the other hand—or paw—looks glad to be home, even if home is a prison. He wags his tail, and whacks it against Johann's arm.

"Poor Johann," murmurs Molly. "I wish we didn't have to do this."

✪ ***Turn to page 142.***

Linda ignores us at Morning Swim, too, and at lunch she twists herself into a pretzel so as not to face us, while studiously avoiding speaking to us. Our activity after lunch is archery, and Linda doesn't even clap when Molly hits the bull's-eye.

Afterward, we're in our tent, changing our clothes for evening inspection. I've just slipped my pin in my pocket when Molly mutters to herself, "Where *is* it?"

"Where's what?" I ask.

"My gold pin," says Molly, scrabbling through her box of stationery. She looks upset. "It's from my Aunt Eleanor, and it means a lot to me. I packed it in this box with my stationery, but now I can't find it."

"Let me help you look," I say. I kneel beside her on the floor and look under the bed.

"Linda," says Molly, looking up, "I know you are mad at me, but have you seen my pin?"

Linda thinks, and then speaks slowly. "I haven't seen it for a while," she says. She looks hard at me, with a challenging frown. "How about you, Margaret?"

"Well, no," I say, puzzled. "I've *never* seen Molly's pin."

"Really?" Linda asks.

Suddenly, I understand. Linda saw me put my pin under my pillow yesterday. She must think *my* pin is *Molly's* pin! I wish I could tell the truth! But I don't want to show either Molly *or* Linda my pin, because if they touch it and rub it by mistake, I don't know *what* might happen.

"I had my pin in my pocket last night," says Molly. "Maybe it fell out of my shorts at dinner. I'll go look in the Dining Hall."

Molly leaves. Linda puts her hands on her hips. "Listen," she says to me, "I didn't say anything to Molly because I'm giving you a chance to come clean. I know you have her pin. I saw you put it under your pillow yesterday. Hand it over."

✪ ***Turn to page 143.***

I speak up. "Gem always says that a dog is a good judge of character. Maxie sure seems to think that Johann is a good guy. So I think that we should think so, too."

"You mean that we should let Johann sneak back into the camp?" Linda asks.

"Yes," I say.

"Me, too," says Molly.

Johann is studying our faces. He looks tense as he wipes sweat off his forehead with the heel of his hand.

Finally Linda says, "Okay." She turns to Johann and then tilts her head toward Molly and me. "Don't worry, Johann," she says. "These two have convinced me not to tell on you. I never like being a snitch, anyway. We're not going to get you in trouble."

"We trust you to go back from here," says Molly, gesturing toward the fence that surrounds the camp."

"Off you go," I say. "Good-bye."

"Auf Wiener schnitzel," says Linda, who's just remembered a German word that she knows.

I know that word, too. Linda is a little mixed up: *wiener schnitzel* is something to eat. It's meat that is breaded and fried!

"Auf Wiedersehen," corrects Molly. She shakes hands with Johann, saying, "So long, pardner."

"Danke," says Johann politely. He scoops Maxie up into his arms, and we watch him sprint to the fence. He lifts a section, shoos Maxie under it, and then crawls back inside the fence himself. Johann turns and gives us one last wave, and then he disappears.

✪ ***Turn to page 145.***

It's a risk I have to take. "It's my fault we were separated from the group," I say again. "I lost something very precious and I had to find it before we could go on. Molly and Linda insisted on staying with me."

"We followed the first rule of hiking," Molly says. "We stuck together."

"Yes," Miss Butternut says. "But you seemed to remember that important rule *after* you got separated from your hiking group." She sighs. "Girls, I'm disappointed in you."

On either side of me, I feel Molly's and Linda's shoulders sag. They feel as badly about disappointing Miss Butternut as I feel about disappointing Gem or Bea. And I feel *terrible* that I'm the cause of all this.

"However," Miss Butternut adds, "I am more impressed with your cooperation, sound decision making, and the responsible leadership each of you showed in a difficult situation."

"You mean," Molly says, "you're not going to send us home?"

Miss Butternut smiles a huge smile. "Oh, heavens no! This is Camp Gowonagin. You learn from your mistakes and 'go on and try again!'"

Miss Archer and Betty smile, too. Molly and Linda and I sigh with relief and hug hard. I'm so glad that everything worked out that I feel like cheering.

✪ ***Turn to page 151.***

Here goes," says Linda. She rattles the fence with both hands and hollers, "Yoo-hoo! Hello? Over here!"

"Who goes there?" comes a thunderous voice. A hefty guard trots toward us with such ferocity that we all shrink back. "Johann!" barks the guard. His frown is as deep and as serious as his voice, which sounds angry. He looks at us, and I realize Molly, Linda, and I must be quite a sight, smeared with mud as we are. "Who are *you*?" he grumbles.

Molly is bravest. "We're from Camp Gowonagin," she says. "We found Maxie hurt and lost in the woods, and Johann found us, and we just thought you should know he's back."

"We know Johann went AWOL," I blurt out anxiously. "But please don't be mad at him. He didn't do any harm. He was just chasing his dog Maxie."

"Come with me," the guard orders Johann and us.

✪ ***Turn to page 149.***

Y ou don't understand," I say desperately.

"Oh, I understand all right," says Linda. "I don't trust you. I'm not surprised you're a thief: You stole my best friend Molly away from me, and now you've stolen Molly's pin away from her."

"That pin you saw is *my* pin," I say. "Or, anyway, I mean, I found it in the woods a few days ago." My explanation sounds lame even to me.

"I know what Molly's pin looks like," says Linda. "If the pin you put under your pillow is not Molly's, I'll apologize. But if it is Molly's pin—and I think it is—then you better give it back. Molly and I are mad at each other right now, but we have been best friends for a long time, and I won't let her get hurt. So," Linda demands, holding out her palm, "show me the pin."

Oh no, oh no! I can't let Linda even *see* the pin. Then she'll want to hold it and inspect it closely to be sure that it isn't Molly's. If she rubs it, I don't know what will happen. My pin might send Linda anywhere in space or time, or it may send her to my home. I can't take the risk.

Home. Suddenly, I long to go back. No one *there* thinks I am a liar and a thief. Everyone trusts me. I slip my hand into my pocket and touch the pin. It's a danger to Linda, but it could be my salvation. Should I just go home now? Or should I stay and try to explain?

✪ ***To stay and explain, turn to page 147.***

✪ ***To go home now, turn to page 157.***

As we turn to go, Linda says, "Johann was pretty nice for a German."

"Johann was pretty nice period," says Molly. She shakes her head in wonderment. "Isn't it weird how war makes us hate people we don't even know? Ever since the war began, newsreels and movies and newspapers and posters have told us that German and Japanese people are terrible. But when we actually meet the enemy, he turns out to be just a regular teenage boy who loves his dog."

"I'm not going to be able to hate *all* German people anymore," says Linda, "now that we've met Johann. *He's* not my enemy."

All this talk about enemies makes me thoughtful as we walk back along the trail that leads to Camp Gowonagin. I realize that I've been treating Mischa like an enemy without really knowing him. I don't like the fact that he's taken over some of the things I do to help Gem. But Mischa doesn't know that. I guess if there's something I really want to keep doing, I should tell him. It's not as if we speak different languages.

"You're awfully quiet, Margaret," Molly says. "What's on your mind?"

"Mischa," I confess.

"The guy at your ranger station?" Linda asks.

"Yes," I say. "I realize I haven't even *tried* to get to know him. Maybe if I stop treating Mischa like a stranger, it'll change how I feel about him."

"I bet it will," says Molly. "Look how getting to know Johann even a little bit changed how we felt about *him*."

"Right," agrees Linda. "So I think getting to know Mischa is worth a try."

It *is* worth a try. And now I know how to do it, too, because Molly and Linda and the other campers showed me. They welcomed me so warmly that instead of feeling awkward or homesick, I felt like a *friend*. I'm ready to go home and get to know Mischa. Oh, but that means that when Molly, Linda, and I get back to Camp Gowonagin, somehow I'll have to tell them I'm leaving! That will be hard. Whether I say "good-bye," or "*auf Wiedersehen*," or even "*auf Wiener schnitzel*," I will miss my wonderful friends forever.

✪ *The End* ✪

To read this story another way and see how different choices lead to a different ending, turn back to page 129.

I can't let Linda or Molly think I'm a thief. I have to stay. I'll just have to figure out some way to keep them from touching my pin.

Slowly, I pull the pin out from my pocket. I hold it up to show it to Linda. She reaches out for it, and—

"I found it!" yells Molly, bursting into the tent. "It was in Lost and Found!" She's so relieved and happy that she impulsively hugs both Linda and me.

Quickly, I put my pin back in my pocket.

Linda looks at me and says, "I'm sorry for what I said."

I smile my forgiveness and say nothing.

But Molly thinks Linda is apologizing for being mad at us. Molly says, "Oh, Linda! I'm sorry, too. You were right: I was bossy. And I should have been more thoughtful of you when I was making friends with Margaret. I got all carried away because I was so wrapped up in learning how to swim underwater."

"Well, it's always good to learn new things," says Linda. She grins at me. "Especially when you have a good teacher you can trust."

"We won't exclude you anymore," says Molly. "I promise."

Now I grin. "It's like that old rhyme," I say. "Make new friends, but keep the old. One is silver, and the other's gold."

"Hey, Linda," says Molly. "For free choice after dinner, maybe you and Bobbie could come swimming with Margaret and me. I'm not afraid to put my head underwater anymore, so I've made a lot of progress with in my diving lessons with Margaret." Molly smiles at me. "Thanks to Margaret, I've decided to go on the fishing trip with Dad. Now I hope I *do* catch the first fish. I can't wait to show Dad that I'm not afraid to dive off the boat." She turns to Linda and says, "It would be great if you and Bobbie could start giving me some diving pointers tonight."

"Okay," says Linda. "We'll give you encouragement, too."

So that's what the four of us do. Every time Molly and I dive off the dock, Linda and Bobbie cheer, which is nice of them because we dive about twenty million times. Well, maybe more like sixty million times!

✪ ***Turn to page 152 .***

We follow the guard around the perimeter—he is on the inside of the fence and we are on the outside—until we reach the gate at the front of the camp. The guard opens the gate, and we file in. The gate swings shut behind us with such a metallic bang that we all jump. As a second guard approaches, Maxie wags his tail and barks a friendly hello. He seems to be happy here.

The second guard shakes his head at Johann and Maxie. "Did you get out again, you bad dog?" he says. But he sounds more amused than angry.

Johann turns to us and says, *"Auf Wiedersehen."* He lifts Maxie's paw, returns Molly's scarf to her, and then waves Maxie's paw to us so that Maxie can say good-bye, too.

"Good-bye, good-bye, Johann!" Molly, Linda, and I say as Johann is led away. "Bye, Maxie!"

"What's going to happen to Johann?" Molly bravely asks the first guard. "Will he be punished?"

"He'll be restricted to camp for the rest of the month," says the guard. "And he'll have extra KP duty."

"What's that?" I ask.

"Kitchen patrol" says the guard. "He will be

washing a lot of dishes in the next few weeks."

"You mean he won't be locked up in handcuffs or put in a cell?" Molly asks. She sounds relieved.

"No. This isn't a jail," says the guard. "The men here aren't criminals; they're soldiers. Some of them can come and go on the honor system as long as they ask permission. Johann must have been so anxious about finding Maxie that he left without asking, and that is not permitted."

"It's impossible to be mad at Maxie, though, isn't it?" says Linda.

"It is," agrees the guard, finally smiling. "We're glad they're both back where they belong. Now let's get you girls back where *you* belong. Come with me."

✪ ***Turn to page 154.***

Miss Butternut sends us back to our tent to clean up, and she gives us free-choice time for the rest of the afternoon. "I know you'll choose wisely," she says cheerfully. "You three are a good team."

"We *are* a good team," says Molly. "We stick together and we help one another."

I think of Bea and how I promised to help her raise Aurora's foal. *Team Moon Shadow,* I think with a heart full of joy. *That's who Bea and I will be. I've decided to stay home this summer, and I can't wait to see what adventures we'll have.*

The End

To read this story another way and see how different choices lead to a different ending, turn back to page 96.

Miss Butternut was right, and so was Linda: All Wet Day is really fun. All of us in Tent Ten are a team in the bucket brigade. We line up next to the team from Tent Eleven, and every girl has a bucket. All the buckets are empty except for the first one. Molly is first in our line. When the whistle blows, she turns and pours the water from her bucket into Linda's bucket, who then pours it into Bobbie's, who then turns and fills Nancy's, and so on down the line. The team that passes the water to the end of its line first wins. There's lots of shrieking and spilling and splashing and laughing. Most of the water sloshes out, so we're all drenched. Our team loses, but it doesn't matter. We're all laughing so hard that we feel like winners anyway!

For the water slide, the counselors have unrolled a long canvas tarp down the steep path to the baseball field and drenched it with water. We sit on trays from the Dining Hall and *swoosh*! Down we all slide, one right after the other, as Miss Archer times us with a stopwatch. Our Tent Ten team wins the waterslide race.

"Our team not only had the fastest time," says Linda, panting and happy, "but we're also the only team whose members actually stayed on the trays without tumbling off, so we're *definitely* the champs!"

The swim meet is more serious. Linda wins second place in the freestyle, and Bobbie wins first in the breaststroke. Guess who wins the Gold Medal for Excellence in the diving competition?

✪ ***Turn to page 162.***

We follow the guard, who says, "I'll call Camp Gowonagin and tell the folks in charge there that you're okay. Then I'll give you a ride back. You can wait inside the library while I make the call."

"You have a library here?" asks Molly.

"And classrooms, and sports fields, and an outdoor stage that the prisoners built to put on concerts and shows," says the guard. "We have lots of musicians here." He leads us inside the library, where it is cool and quiet. "Shh!" he says.

He leaves to call Camp Gowonagin, and we look around the library. Men are writing letters and reading. When the guard returns, we follow him and climb into a jeep.

As we ride home, jouncing in the jeep, the guard explains, "Now that the war is over in Europe, enemy soldiers are surrendering or being captured by the thousands. There's no space or food for them in England, so they're shipped over here. There are seven hundred prisoner of war camps here in the U.S., and nearly half a million prisoners."

"Wow," Molly, Linda, and I say.

"Half a *million*?" asks Linda, astounded. "I didn't

know that. I bet most other people don't either. Are the camps top secret?"

"No," says the guard. "Communities near them know about them, because the prisoners often work outside the camps doing construction projects like building reservoirs and bridges, and harvesting on farms and orchards and vineyards. They do work that needs to be done because our own women and men are away fighting."

"Johann's more of a boy than a man," says Molly. "Isn't he awfully young to be a soldier?"

"Lots of these boys didn't have a choice, really," says the guard. "They were conscripted, which means they had to join the German army. Some were threatened with death, or their families were threatened with harm, if they didn't sign up."

"What will happen to them now?" I ask.

"They'll be shipped back home, eventually," says the guard. "Speaking of home, here you are, ladies, home at Camp Gowonagin." The guard stops the jeep on the main road, at the turnoff for the camp.

"Thank you," we say in a chorus. As I climb out, I realize how tired I am. Molly and Linda look beat, too.

We hardly talk as we finish the last part of our hike. Slowly, silently, we trudge down the road to Camp Gowonagin.

"We didn't get to see the secret pond," Linda says.

"No," Molly answers. "But we did see something important and unforgettable, didn't we?"

✪ ***Turn to page 160.***

I didn't take Molly's pin, Linda," I say. "I hope somehow you find out that's true."

Linda frowns. Before she says a word, I fly out of the tent and run as fast as I can to the privacy of a group of trees.

I don't know what happened to Molly's pin. I feel terrible that Linda suspects me of stealing it. Unless she finds it, Molly may suspect me of stealing it, too. I do *not* want to leave like this. But it's the safest option.

I rub the pin, and *whoosh*. I am back in my own woods. I'm shaking, out of breath, and heartbroken to have left Molly and Linda, especially because they think I took something that doesn't belong to me.

But I am *home*.

I trudge toward our cabin, weighed down by having been judged unfairly. It feels awful to be accused of stealing, and I hate that I had to leave camp before I was forgiven for something I didn't do. I also feel awful that I came between Molly and Linda. I never, *ever* meant to make Linda feel left out.

Something nags at my conscience. There's someone *I've* blamed for making me feel left out. Someone whom I have judged unfairly.

As I walk into the clearing around our cabin, I hear the familiar sound of whimpering. It's the sound Barney makes when he has to sit still. I see Mischa hard at work, trying to keep Barney still so he can pick the burrs out of his coat. Barney squirms and barks when he sees me.

"Hi there, Margaret," Mischa says cheerfully. "How was your walk?"

"Fine," I say quietly.

Mischa looks at me, and then at Barney. "Maybe Barney would like it better if you did this. I know he's your dog." Mischa sounds apologetic.

Mischa hasn't done anything wrong. *It's time I started treating Mischa with some kindness, the way I was treated kindly by everyone I met at Camp Gowonagin,* I think. *I shouldn't resent him for just being here.* I hold both hands up. "That's okay," I say. "In fact, thank you for doing that yucky job."

Mischa looks a little surprised. Then he says, "I could use some help. Please, will you distract Barney? He's got an especially sticky burr I can't get out."

"Okay," I say. I kneel down in front of Barney and rub his nose, right where he likes it. He licks my hand gratefully. *I'm forgiving Mischa for being here,* I think, *and he's forgiving me for my unfriendliness.* My heart lightens a bit. Somehow, our mutual forgiveness gives me hope that maybe Linda and Molly have found Molly's pin and they are forgiving me right now, too.

✪ *The End* ✪

To read this story another way and see how different choices lead to a different ending, turn back to page 143.

Yes," Linda says slowly. "But I don't know what to think. These guys—boys like Johann—were our enemies. They were fighting against our American soldiers. The Germans have done terrible things. They've killed millions of innocent people, especially Jewish people. Are we supposed to be the Germans' friends now, and forgive and forget?"

"I don't think we *should* forget," says Molly. "And I'm not sure some things can—or should—ever be forgiven."

I think about how I've been so worried about Bea's forgiving me if I go to music camp. That seems like such a small matter now, compared to Molly and Linda's worries. They lived through a war! The questions they have about forgiveness are difficult, maybe even impossible, to answer. Now I understand what Molly's dad meant when he said that camp is a good break because the war is hard on kids, too. I admire Molly and Linda, and I'm inspired by how they've kept open minds and hearts when it comes to forgiveness.

When we reach the Recreation Hall, Molly and Linda start walking toward the office to tell Miss Butternut that we're back safe and sound. But I stop them. "Hey," I say. "Listen. I'm going home now."

"What?" Molly and Linda say, looking surprised.

"I've got to ask someone to forgive me," I say. Even though it's a small matter, it's important to me.

"Bea?" Molly asks.

I nod.

"She will," Molly assures me. "She's your friend, and friends forgive each other."

"I'll never forget how much I've learned from both of you," I say. "Or how kind you've been to me."

"How will you get home?" asks Linda.

I pat my pocket. "I've got my ticket right here," I say. "I've had it all along. I've just been very 'Margaret Maybe' about deciding to use it."

"We'll never forget you, Margaret," says Molly. "There's absolutely no maybe about that."

"Good-bye!" Molly, Linda, and I say to one another.

As I walk away, my heart is full of sadness about leaving, happiness about going home, and most of all, gratitude for my wonderful experience with Molly and Linda. There's absolutely no maybe about *that* either.

✪ ***Turn to page 163.***

I do. Molly and Linda laugh when they see my stunned expression.

"It was all those millions of dives you did when you were teaching me," says Molly. "You were practicing without even realizing it! No wonder you won."

"Congratulations," Linda says, patting me on the back. "And congratulations to you, too, Molly, for winning the award for most improved swimmer."

"Thanks," says Molly. "I was *dolphinately* surprised!"

I look at the gold medal. It glows in the sun. Once again, the old rhyme comes into my mind: Make new friends, but keep the old. One is silver, and the other's gold.

Old friends are important, and not to be taken for granted. If I go to music camp, I'll make new friends, and some may turn out to be silver. But Molly and Linda will always be pure gold, and they have shown me that no matter what I decide, I've got to be sure Bea knows that she's pure gold, too, and always will be.

✪ *The End* ✪

To read this story another way and see how different choices lead to a different ending, turn back to page 22.

I watch Molly and Linda disappear around the Dining Hall. Then I duck behind one of the big trees and take the pin out of my pocket. I take a deep breath, rub the white stone, and *whoosh*! First darkness, then light, then I am back in the woods—*my* woods—sitting on the rotted step. I hold the pin in my palm, thinking: *We share a secret, don't we?*

I set off for Bea's house. The woods smell piney, and the gentle breeze at my back helps me on my way.

I hear Bea before I see her in the paddock. She's singing to Moon Shadow:

And the green grass grew all around, all around,
and the green grass grew all around.

She stops singing when she sees me. "Hi," she says.

"Bea," I begin.

At the exact same time we both say, "I'm sorry."

"What?" I say. "Why are you sorry?"

"I wasn't very understanding about your music camp news," Bea says. "I was too busy freaking out about you being gone instead of thinking how much you'd love it. I'm sorry I acted that way."

I apologize to Bea. "And I'm sorry for changing our summer plans," I say. "I would never miss out on Moon Shadow's first few weeks if it wasn't really important."

"I know you wouldn't," says Bea. "I forgive you." She doesn't know it, but she quotes Molly as she says, "That's what friends do, right?"

✪ ***The End*** ✪

To read this story another way and see how different choices lead to a different ending, turn back to page 22.

INSIDE Molly's World

During World War Two, it was hard for an American family to take a vacation together. Many fathers were away fighting in the war, and mothers were working in factories, making war supplies. So lots of children took vacations without their families at summer camp.

In the 1940s, summer camps were like large parks in the woods, on lakes, or near the ocean. They were built as places for children to study nature and have fun outdoors. Campers cooked over open fires. They lived in tents without electricity, so at night they used flashlights. They had only cold water and used outhouses rather than indoor plumbing. All of these things made campers like Molly feel as if they were living in the wilderness.

In fact, learning wilderness skills was one of the most popular parts of camp life. Campers practiced starting a fire with only one match and built shelters using only a blanket or pine boughs and a few sticks. They studied pictures of wild animal tracks and learned which woodland plants were poisonous and which were safe to eat.

Of course children like Molly weren't living in the wilderness. Cooks made most of their meals, and counselors were there to take care of the campers. They had tents and cabins to live in, and wild animals were nowhere close by.

During World War Two, campers were proudly patriotic. Every day began and ended with the Pledge of Allegiance and flag ceremony. Many things about camp life reminded campers of what their fathers told them about life in the military. Campers wore uniforms, and they lived together in groups like soldiers. Six or eight of them shared a tent or a cabin. They were responsible for keeping it clean and had daily inspections to see if their beds were made properly and their belongings were tidy. Although camps were often run like the military, the focus was on fun. Days were full of arts and crafts, sports, swimming and boating, games, and singing so that children could take a break from the worries of war.

The war created a very different kind of camp in America. From 1942 to 1945, more than 400,000 prisoners lived in 700 camps all across the United States. The U.S. government worried that the presence of the enemy—especially Germans—would cause fear among civilians, so news reports about the camps were limited. Although some people were upset, the prisoners of war, or POWs, provided a valuable service. Because so many men and women were doing war work, there was a shortage of labor, especially in agricultural industries. POWs were paid to pick fruits and vegetables and work in canning factories—often alongside local residents.

Many German prisoners became friends with the Americans with whom they worked. When the war ended and POWs were sent home, thousands returned to live in America. Some even married women they'd met while working outside POW camps.

Read more of MOLLY'S stories,

available from booksellers and at *americangirl.com*

Classics

Molly's classic series, now in two volumes:

Volume 1:

A Winning Spirit

Life on the home front is full of challenges. Molly does her best to make do with less and help the war effort. Missing Dad, who is far away in England, is the hardest sacrifice of all!

Volume 2:

Stars, Stripes, and Surprises

Even allies have arguments sometimes. Molly learns to get along with new friends as well as forever friends, with some surprises along the way.

Journey in Time

Travel back in time—and spend a day with Molly!

Chances and Changes

Take a trip to Camp Gowonagin with Molly! Go on an overnight nature hike, compete in the swim meet, and discover fun camp traditions. Choose your own path through this multiple-ending story.

A Sneak Peek at

A Winning Spirit

A Molly Classic
Volume 1

Molly's adventures begin in the first volume of her classic stories.

Molly McIntire sat at the kitchen table daydreaming about her Halloween costume. It would be a pink dress with a long, floaty skirt that would swirl when she turned and swish when she walked. There would be shiny silver stars on the skirt to match the stars in her crown. The top of the dress would be white. Maybe it would be made of fluffy angora, only Molly wasn't sure they had angora back in Cinderella's time. That's who Molly wanted to be for Halloween—Cinderella. All she had to do was:

1. talk her mother into buying the material and making the costume,
2. find some glass slippers somewhere, and
3. convince Linda and Susan, her two best friends, to be the ugly stepsisters.

She could probably talk Susan into it. As long as Susan got to wear a long dress, she wouldn't mind being a stepsister. But Linda was another story. If they were going to be fairy-tale princesses, Linda would want to be Snow White because she had black hair just like Snow White's. Linda would want Molly and Susan to be dwarfs. *Probably Sleepy and Grumpy,* thought Molly.

Well, Molly certainly felt like Grumpy tonight. She looked at the clock. She had been sitting at the kitchen table for exactly two hours, forty-six minutes, and one, two, three seconds. She had been sitting at the kitchen table, in fact, ever since six o'clock, when Mrs. Gilford, the housekeeper, called everyone to supper.

Molly had smelled trouble as soon as she walked into the kitchen. It was a heavy, hot smell, kind of like the smell of dirty socks. She sat down and saw the odd orange heap on her plate. She made up her mind right away not to eat it. "What's this orange stuff?" she asked.

Mrs. Gilford turned around and gave her what Molly's father used to call the Gladys Gilford Glacial Glare. "Polite children do not refer to food as *stuff*," said Mrs. Gilford. "The vegetable which you are lucky enough to have on your plate is mashed turnip."

"I'd like to *re*turn it," whispered Molly's twelve-year-old brother Ricky.

"What was that, young man?" asked Mrs. Gilford sharply.

"I like to *eat* turnips," said Ricky, and he shoveled a forkful into his mouth. Eating turnips—or anything alive or dead—was no hardship for Ricky. If it could be chewed, Ricky would eat it. Quick as a wink, all his turnips were gone.

That rat Ricky, thought Molly. She looked over at her older sister, Jill. Jill was putting ladylike bites of turnip in her mouth and washing them down with long, quiet sips of water. Almost all of the horrible orange stuff was gone from her plate.

Molly sighed. In the old days, before Jill turned fourteen and got stuck-up, Molly used to be able to count on her to make a big fuss about things like turnips. But lately, Molly had to do it all herself. Jill was acting superior. This new grown-up Jill was a terrible disappointment to Molly. If that's what happened to you when you got to be fourteen, Molly would rather be nine forever.

The turnips sat on Molly's plate getting cold. They were turning into a solid lump that oozed water. With her fork, Molly carefully pushed her meat and potatoes to a corner of her plate so that not a speck of turnip would touch them and ruin them. "Disgusting," she said softly.

"There will be no such language used at this table,"

said Mrs. Gilford. "Furthermore, anyone who fails to finish her turnips will have no dessert. Nor will she be allowed to leave the table until the turnips are gone."

That's why Molly was still at the kitchen table facing a plate of cold turnips at 8:46 P.M. *None of this would have happened if Dad were home,* she thought. Molly touched the heart-shaped locket she wore on a thin chain around her neck. She pulled it forward and opened it up to look at the tiny picture inside. Her father's face smiled back at her.

Molly's father was a doctor. When American soldiers started fighting in World War Two, he joined the army. Now he was somewhere in England, taking care of wounded and sick soldiers. He had been gone for seven months. Molly missed him every single minute of every single day, but especially at dinnertime.

Before Dad left, before the war, Molly's family never ate supper in the kitchen. They ate dinner in the dining room. Before Dad left, back before the war, the whole family always had dinner together. They laughed and talked the whole time. Now things were different. Dad was gone, and every morning Molly's mother went off to work at the Red Cross headquarters. Very often she got home too late to have dinner with the family. And she spent at least an hour every night writing to Dad.

When a letter came from Dad, it was a surprise and a treat. Everyone gathered and listened in silence while Mrs. McIntire read the letter aloud. Dad always sent a special message to each member of the family. He told jokes and drew funny sketches of himself. But he didn't say which hospital he worked in or name any of the towns he visited. That wasn't allowed, because of the war. And even though Dad's letters were long and funny and wonderful, they still sounded as if they came from very far away. They were not at all like the words Dad spoke in his deep-down voice that you could feel rumbling inside you and filling up the house. Molly used to be able to hear that voice even when she was up in her room doing homework.

When Dad called out, "I'm home!" the house seemed more lively. Everyone, even Jill, would tumble down the stairs for a big hug. Then Dad would sit in his old plaid chair, cozy in a warm circle of lamplight, and they'd tell him what had gone on in school that day. Dad's pipe smoke made the room smell of vanilla and burning leaves. Sometimes, now that Dad was gone to the war, Molly would climb into the plaid chair and sniff it because that vanilla pipe smell made her feel so safe and happy, just as if Dad were home.

Molly remembered the fun they had at the dinner table when Dad was home. He teased Jill and made her blush. He swapped jokes with Ricky and told riddles to Brad, Molly's younger brother. And he always said, "Gosh and golly, olly Molly, what have *you* done today?" Suddenly, everything Molly had done—whether it was winning a running race or losing a multiplication bee—was interesting and important, wonderful or not so bad after all.

Dad loved to tease Mrs. Gilford, too. As she carried steaming trays out from the kitchen with lots of importance, Dad would say, "Mrs. Gladys Gilford, an advancement has been made tonight in the art of cooking. Never before in the history of mankind has there been such a perfect pot roast." Mrs. Gilford would beam and bustle and serve up more perfect pot roast and mashed potatoes and gravy. She never, ever, served anything awful like turnips.

But everything was different now because of the war. Dad was gone and Mom was busy at the Red

Cross. So Mrs. Gilford, who had arrived at the dot of seven o'clock every weekday morning of Molly's life to cook and clean, now ruled the roost more than ever. And Mrs. Gilford was determined to do her part to help win the war.

A Victory garden was Mrs. Gilford's latest war effort. Last spring she sent away for a pamphlet called *Food Fights for Freedom.* It explained how to start a Victory garden in your own backyard. The pamphlet had a picture of vegetables lined up in front of a potato and an onion that were wearing military hats and saluting. Under the picture it said "Call vegetables into service."

"From now on, there will be no more canned vegetables used in this house," Mrs. Gilford announced. "The soldiers need the tin in those cans more than we do. From now on, we will grow, preserve, and eat our own vegetables. It's the least we can do for our fighting boys."

All summer long, Mrs. Gilford had tended her Victory garden. She wore a stiff straw hat, Dr. McIntire's gardening gloves, and knee-high black rubber boots. Everyone, even little Brad, had helped her.

Molly had worked in the Victory garden every Tuesday morning from ten to eleven o'clock. She had crawled on her hands and knees through rows of green seedlings, pulling weeds. The rows were as strict and straight as soldiers on parade. Each one was labeled with a colorful seed packet on a stake. The seed packets showed fat carrots, plump red tomatoes, and big green peas.

But by fall, after months in the hot sun, the pictures on the seed packets had faded away. The packets hung on the stakes like limp white flags of surrender. Mrs. Gilford's Victory garden had not been quite as victorious as she had hoped. All but the toughest vegetables had been beaten by the dry summer. The carrots were thin and wrinkled. The tomatoes were as hard as nuts. The peas were brown. But that did not defeat Mrs. Gilford. She would never give up and open a tin can. She had a rather successful crop of radishes, lima beans, and turnips, so that's what they would eat.

About the Author

VALERIE TRIPP says that she became a writer because of the kind of person she is. She says she's curious, and writing requires you to be interested in everything. Talking is her favorite sport, and writing is a way of talking on paper. She's a daydreamer, which helps her come up with ideas. And she loves words. She even loves the struggle to come up with the right words as she writes and rewrites. Ms. Tripp lives in Maryland with her husband.